THE BAG OF BONES

The Second Tale from
THE FIVE KINGDOMS

THE BAG OF BONES

VIVIAN FRENCH

ILLUSTRATED BY ROSS COLLINS

CANDLEWICK PRESS

Text copyright © 2008 by Vivian French
Illustrations copyright © 2008 by Ross Collins

First U.S. edition 2009

Library of Congress Cataloging-in-Publication Data is available.

Library of Congress Catalog Card Number 2008938423

ISBN 978-0-7636-4255-6

2 4 6 8 10 9 7 5 3 1

Printed in the United States of America

This book was typeset in Baskerville.

Candlewick Press
99 Dover Street
Somerville, Massachusetts 02144

visit us at www.candlewick.com

For Jessie
with lots of love

PRINCIPAL CHARACTERS

Gracie Gillypot . . . . a Trueheart
Truda Hangnail . . . . a wicked witch
Loobly Higgins . . . . an orphan
Marlon . . . . a bat
Alf . . . . Marlon's nephew
Gubble . . . . a troll
Buckleup Brandersby . . . Master-in-Charge of the Happy
Times Orphanage
Queen Bluebell . . . . Queen of Wadingburn
Prince Arioso . . . . heir to the kingdom of Gorebreath
Prince Marcus . . . . his twin

THE WITCHES OF WADINGBURN

Evangeline Droop . . . . . the Grand High Witch of
Wadingburn
Mrs. Prag
Mrs. Vibble
Mrs. Cringe
Ms. Scurrilous

THE ANCIENT CRONES

Edna . . . . the Ancient One
Elsie . . . . the Oldest
Val . . . . the Youngest

ASSORTED RATS

Brother Bodalisk
Brother Brokenbiscuit
Brother Burwash
Doily
Sprout

Chapter One

"Wheeeeee!" The small bat did a double backflip, then a twist, and landed neatly on the branch below. "Did you see me, Uncle Marlon? Did you *SEE* me?" Alf squeaked.

"Shh!" The older bat flapped a warning wing. "Button up, kiddo. We've got company." He stared into the night. "Hmph. It's those dames from Wadingburn."

The small bat's eyes widened. "The *witches*? Oh, Uncle Marlon! Can we stay 'n' watch? Will they do scary spells?"

"They're no big deal, kiddo." The older bat settled back on his branch. "Deep Magic's not allowed in the Five Kingdoms. This lot are Shallow, through and through. Couldn't magic a bird off a branch. But keep mum, all the same. You don't want to end up in a pot. Your ma'll kill me if I bring you back half-boiled."

The small bat shivered, half in fear, half with pleasure. "Okeydokey, Uncle M." And he froze into still-
ness as he watched the line of women, varying in shape
and size but all dressed in black, making their way into
the clearing at the top of Wadingburn Hill. Limping
at the end of the line was the small, skinny figure of
a girl, her head bent tenderly over the bundle in her
arms. As the witches hurried here and there, collecting
firewood and setting up the old and dented black cauldron, she slipped away and settled herself at the foot
of the tree where the two bats hung motionless. Softly
she began to croon to the bundled-up object she was
holding, rocking it gently to and fro.

"Loobly Higgins!" said a terrible voice. "What on
EARTH do you think you're doing?"

Loobly jumped. "N-n-n-nothing, Auntie," she
quavered.

The Grand High Witch of Wadingburn took a
step closer. "Did my eyes deceive me, or were you
KISSING that rat?"

Loobly shook her head so hard that her long,
stringy hair broke loose from its ribbon and fell over
her thin little face. "Wasn't kissing it," she whispered.
"Not kissing. Just telling sorry. Sorry it be picklified."

The Grand High Witch sighed in exasperation. "It'll be no use now. No use at all. How many times do I have to tell you to leave my ingredients alone?"

"Sorry, Auntie Levangeline. Loobly hear you. Loobly very sorry." Loobly pushed the hair out of her eyes and looked up hopefully. "If no use, can Loobly keep he?"

"Certainly NOT!" The witch was on the point of snatching the rat away when she was distracted by the sound of cackling laughter. Instantly forgetting Loobly, she turned to see her five fellow witches gathering around the cauldron that was now bubbling gently in the center of the clearing. At once the Grand High Witch drew herself to her full height and strode forward to greet them.

"*Dear* Mrs. Cringe! I'm so glad you're with us tonight! *And* Mrs. Vibble and Mrs. Prag as well. Fabulous! And darling Ms. Scurrilous is here too! *And* Mrs. . . . ."

The Grand High Witch faltered for a moment. What was the name of the hunched old witch on the far side of the fire? Even with the flames now burning brightly under the cauldron, it was too dark to see her face. It certainly wasn't Mrs. Gabbage, and Ms. Pettigroan had sent a bat earlier that evening with polite apologies.

Mrs. Cringe shuffled up, looking distinctly guilty,

and the Grand High Witch's heart sank. Even worse, her little toe had begun to throb, which was a far more reliable warning of impending trouble. She had always been wary of Mrs. Cringe, not least because she was known to have relations outside the Five Kingdoms who were suspected of indulging in Deep Magic of the nastiest kind.

"Ahem," Mrs. Cringe addressed the Grand High Witch, whose toe was becoming increasingly painful. "That there's my grandmother, Truda Hangnail. She's come visiting from the other side of the More Enchanted Forest. Asked if I could invite her in for a week or two. Things got troublesome for her over there, she said. Too many two-headed cows and sheep with five legs appearing all over the place." She stepped closer and dropped her voice to a whisper. "Best to be polite. She's in a bit of a temper. Fell in a ditch on the other side of the border gate." She nudged the Grand High Witch. "Shouldn't even be here in the Five Kingdoms. Deep, she is. Very Deep. But we won't tell, will we?"

Evangeline Droop, Grand High Witch of Wadingburn, froze. It was a serious offense to invite a Deep Witch to cross the border of the Five Kingdoms. They had been banished many years before, together with werewolves and sorcerers. On the other hand, she had absolutely no idea how to confront a Deep Witch, let alone how to tell her to go home.

Evangeline's little toe was now excruciating. All the same, she extended an unwilling hand and said as gracefully as she was able, "Delighted to meet you, Mrs. Hangnail!"

The visitor stared at her with beady little eyes, and the strangely sinuous animal draped around her neck lifted its head and stared too. "Deep or Shallow?" the witch croaked.

Mrs. Cringe took her elderly relation by the arm. "I told you, Grandma. There aren't any Deep Witches in the Five Kingdoms."

Truda Hangnail gave a laugh like knives scraping steel. "There's no fun in that," she sneered. "You can't turn princes into toads with Shallow Magic. How d'you put red-hot nails in a milkmaid's shoes? And how d'you scare folk into giving you plump young chickens and apple pies and bowls of eggs and dishes of cream?"

"Actually, Mrs. Hangnail," the Grand High Witch said haughtily, "we are respected members of our community."

Mrs. Prag looked smug. "We've all been invited to

Queen Bluebell's eightieth-birthday party to hear the Declaration."

"It's a Declaration Ball, Vera," Mrs. Vibble corrected her. "*Do* get it right."

"*So* exciting!" Ms. Scurrilous beamed with pleasure. "We'll be among the very first to know who she's chosen as her successor!"

Truda stiffened like a fox who has seen a foolish young rabbit. Even her nose sharpened. "Successor?"

Ms. Scurrilous heaved a romantic sigh. "So sad. Her daughter ran away, and there's only a grandson. And of course we don't have kings in Wadingburn, so it's been a terrible worry."

"Serves the old bag right," Truda snapped.

"Excuse *me*, Mrs. Hangnail!" Evangeline's voice rose several octaves. "You are speaking of our beloved monarch!"

"Oooh — beg your pardon, I'm sure." The old witch bobbed a sarcastic curtsy. "So what else do you do, besides visiting royalty?"

Mrs. Vibble bridled. "We offer charms and soothing cures for the afflicted."

"That's right," Ms. Scurrilous added. "And we get paid for our work without frightening anyone."

"YAH!" Truda stuck out her long green tongue.

"Mimsy-whimsy sort of stuff. Cough drops and love potions as well, I'll be bound." She hobbled toward the bubbling cauldron and peered inside. "Just as I thought. Moldy mushrooms, shriveled spiders' legs, chicken soup, and nail clippings. Call yourselves witches? Spineless old hags is what you are! Now, let me see . . ." She began to fish in the pockets of her shabby old cloak, then pulled out a tattered cloth bag. "Frog bones, bat bones, rat bones, cat bones . . . How about a few dragon bones to begin with? Nicely ground into dust, of course."

Mrs. Prag grabbed Evangeline's arm. "What's she doing?" she hissed. "Stop her! Dragon bones are illegal!"

Evangeline swallowed hard. As Grand High Witch of Wadingburn, voted into the post by every witch in the kingdom, she knew she should take command. She should order this terrible old hag to go, scat, vamoose, and refuse to take no for an answer. But there had been something in Truda Hangnail's eyes that was making Evangeline feel oddly indecisive.

"Erm . . ." she began. "We don't usually use those kinds of ingredients."

"You don't, eh?" Truda sneered. "Well, could be

it's time you did. I'm thinking we could have some fun and games in this cozy little kingdom of yours. I'm thinking we could make it a tad more exciting. Could just be I've found something worth staying for!" She gave an evil cackle, opened the bag, and tossed a handful of gray dust into the cauldron.

Nothing happened.

Truda swore and gave the cauldron a sharp kick.

At once there was a flash, and a cloud of thick purple smoke rose up and swirled around Truda's shoulders before spreading across the clearing. The witches of Wadingburn coughed and spluttered, and Evangeline felt her eyes sting and water. Strange thoughts raced into her mind; she remembered how only that morning the butcher's boy had accidentally ridden across a corner of her flower bed, and she was suddenly seized with a burning desire to raise a huge red boil on the end of his nose.

"Do it! Do it!" Truda Hangnail was standing right in front of her. "Let the evil do its work! Let wickedness rule! You call yourself a Grand High Witch — so make folk suffer! Take the power and follow me!"

Evangeline swallowed. On the other side of the cauldron, Mrs. Prag and Mrs. Vibble had linked arms and were muttering curses. Mrs. Cringe and Ms. Scurrilous were scowling terrible scowls and making threatening gestures as they stamped up and down.

Truda pointed a withered finger at Mrs. Cringe. "Granddaughter of mine," she intoned, "you brought me here. Come to the cauldron and take the power of the Deep Magic . . . you and all who are in this place. Let the Deep Magic return to Wadingburn . . . Deep, Deep, *Deep* Magic!" And she strode to the seething cauldron and held out her bony hand. Mrs. Cringe, moving like a sleepwalker, drifted inexorably toward the hand and took it. Ms. Scurrilous followed and was grasped by Mrs. Cringe. Mrs. Prag and Mrs. Vibble, hand in hand like schoolgirls, joined themselves to the chain, and the Grand High Witch felt an acute longing to join them. Her head was swirling with wicked thoughts and the desire for power, but there was still a part of her that knew this was not her true self, that this was the wish of Truda Hangnail.

"Don't go! Oh, Auntie Levangeline, don't go handling hold!"

The small squeaky voice cut through the confusion in Evangeline's mind, and she stopped. Loobly was dancing up and down in agitation, still clutching the

rat. "Smell badness," she shrilled. "*Bad* badness, Auntie! Loobly knows it is!"

With a last desperate effort, Evangeline, Grand High Witch of Wadingburn, spoke as her real self. "Loobly!" She gasped. "Loobly . . . go to the crones . . . the Ancient Crones . . ." and then she was sucked into the purple mist.

Chapter Two

Gracie Gillypot sat up in bed with a start. Someone or something was in her room, and it was scratching on the walls.

"Is—is anyone there?" Gracie asked, hoping her voice wasn't trembling. It wasn't that she was nervous, she told herself, it was more that she wasn't quite sure what was happening. The House of the Ancient Crones had a curious habit of swapping parts of itself every so often, so that the front door would suddenly pop up on the roof, or on a side wall, or even in the cellar. Gracie had lost her bedroom two or three times since she had moved in, but fortunately there was a sign on the door saying HEDGEHOGS ONLY, so she had been able to track it down among the many other doors that played hide-and-seek up and down the corridors. The kitchen was particularly inclined to slide from one end of the building to the other; only room seventeen remained more or less in the same place. This was fortunate, as it was the room where the crones kept their two old-fashioned but all-important looms. On one they created fine pieces of cloth that were made into robes of skulls, or cloaks of invisibility, or whatever else might be ordered (and paid for at a quite exorbitant rate; "We are not," the Ancient One frequently remarked, "a charity."). Shimmering on the taller loom was the silver web that held the balance between Good and Evil, and here work never stopped. Day and night alike the Youngest, the Oldest, or the Ancient One sat steadily weaving. Gracie had offered to help and had been allowed a couple of minutes now and then, but never longer. The Newest was forbidden to touch the fragile silver threads at all; she was in the process of being trained in the ways of the Ancient Crones and was, as yet, highly unreliable.

"It'll be a good few years before she's properly drained of evil," the Youngest had told Gracie when the Newest first arrived. "Took me long enough, and I wasn't anything like such a Falseheart as her. She's the worst the Ancient One's ever taken on." Then suddenly remembering that the Newest was Gracie's stepsister, the Youngest looked awkward. "That is, I'm sure she had moments of being nice. . . ."

"She didn't," Gracie said with feeling. "It's OK, Auntie Val. She was *dreadful.*" And the conversation had been dropped, and the Youngest went back to her weaving.

The scratching continued.

Gracie felt on her bedside table for the matches and, after a couple of attempts, finally managed to light her candle. Holding it high, she peered around the room . . . and saw a quill pen spattering ink in all directions as it wrote furiously on the whitewashed walls.

"Oh," Gracie said with relief. "It's only you."

The pen paused momentarily, then started off again.

Gracie yawned. "Couldn't you do that in the morning? Is it really important?"

The pen shot across the room, wrote YES YES YES! on the wall above her head, then zoomed back to continue its scrawl. Gracie sighed and swung her legs over the edge of her bed. Only the week before, the pen had spent a whole afternoon drawing big fat hearts on her ceiling together with a banner inscribed GRACIE LOVES MARCUS. Gracie hadn't been pleased, partly because this was a very private matter, and partly because it had taken her a whole morning to wash it off.

"What is it now?" She picked up the candle, and walked over to read what the pen had written.

"DANGER HELP HELP DANGER," she read. "GO GO GO . . ." And then the same again, over and over.

"Please—" Gracie was always polite, even to a quill pen that had woken her at midnight. "Please . . . couldn't you give me a bit more information?"

The pen spluttered, wrote URGENT! and shot off under the door. Gracie looked after it in resigned exasperation.

"I'd better go and ask one of the aunties," she decided, pulling on her bathrobe. "And maybe I'll make myself a cup of tea at the same time."

She opened her bedroom door, stepped out into the corridor, and set off for the kitchen. A second later she found herself facing the front door, which opened itself invitingly, letting in a great deal of cold night air.

"No, thanks," Gracie said. "I'm going to have a cup of tea and a chat with whoever's on the loom." She turned around and set off in the other direction. The House gave a convulsive shake, and yet again she was looking through the open door at the dark night outside.

Gracie folded her arms. "Look," she said. "I get the message. I know you want me to go—but I'm still in my pajamas, it's the middle of the night, and I want to talk to Auntie Edna or Auntie Elsie. If I promise I'll leave right afterward, will you let me go and find them?"

There was a curious heaving along the floorboards, and the House settled down.

"Thank you." Gracie took a deep breath, turned around yet again, and hurried along the corridor until she found the door marked WATER WINGS. Once inside, she sighed with relief as she found the kitchen exactly the same as it always was and went about the business of boiling a kettle and making tea for two.

"Three," said a voice from a cupboard.

"OK, Gubble," Gracie said cheerfully. "Tea for three." She filled the teapot, poured out a cupful, and added milk and four sugars.

"Five?" The voice was hopeful.

Gracie shook her head. "Not good for you." Leaving the cup on the table, she put the other two cups on a tray and made her way to room seventeen, where the Oldest was steadily weaving. The second loom was neatly packed up for the night; a length of sky-blue velvet lay on it, and Gracie smoothed it lovingly as she walked past.

"Pretty, isn't it?" said the Oldest as she pushed her wig of bright red curls farther back on her head. "Shame it's for Princess Nina-Rose; it'd suit you nicely. Just the thing for a pretty girl at her first ball. Although I don't know why Queen Bluebell's calling it a Declaration Ball, exactly, seeing as her daughter ran away years ago."

Gracie smiled, trying hard not to look as if she were sorry for herself. "I told you, Auntie Elsie. Queen Bluebell's not going to ask me. The ball's this coming Saturday, and I haven't had an invitation. I've brought you some tea."

"That's very nice of you, dear," Elsie said, and she patted Gracie's hand. "Shouldn't you be in bed, though?"

"I was." Gracie busied herself with the cups. "But . . . but the quill's been writing things all over my walls. I came to ask you about it. It wrote DANGER, and HELP, and URGENT!—and the House is desperate for me to go somewhere, but I don't know where. What do you think?"

The Oldest didn't answer. She had turned back to the loom and was staring at the fine cloth in front of her.

Gracie, peering over her shoulder, saw a dark

purple stain spreading across the silver. "What's that?" she asked.

"That," said the Oldest grimly, "is Trouble."

"Oh." Gracie rubbed her nose thoughtfully. "What sort of trouble?"

The Oldest Crone looked again at the stain. "Magic, I'd say. And Deep Magic at that. The very nastiest sort of magic. Oh, dearie, dearie me. That's dreadful. I wonder where it could be coming from?"

"That must have been what the quill was writing about." Gracie was conscious of a cold chill creeping into her stomach. "No wonder the House is so upset." She swallowed hard. "It really, *really* wants me to go . . . and if I leave now, I could be in the Five Kingdoms by midday. It's market day in Gorebreath, so if anything odd's been happening, somebody there's sure to know." She didn't add that her stomach was now feeling as if it were full of whirling butterflies and that she wouldn't have the faintest idea what to do if she met up with any Deep Magic. Neither had she any idea how to recognize it if she *did* meet it. "And then . . . then I suppose I could come back here to tell you?"

The Oldest wasn't listening. She was studying the web intently. "That sounds very sensible, dear," she said vaguely. "Now, should I wake the Ancient One

at once or leave it until the morning when Val arrives and we can discuss it together? What we need to know is, has it reached the Five Kingdoms . . ."

"I'll try to find out," Gracie promised, and she hurried out of room seventeen to get dressed before the enormity of what she was about to do made her change her mind.

The House, however, had other ideas. As Gracie reached the corridor, it tipped itself up, and she found herself sliding inexorably toward the front door. This time she could do nothing to save herself, and before she could shout or scream, she was outside sitting on the front path. With a wriggle of excitement, the path picked itself and Gracie up, swung around toward the front gate, and deposited Gracie neatly on the other side.

"Ooof!" Gracie tried to catch her breath.

A second later the top of the path reappeared, and a large, solid figure was unceremoniously dumped on the ground beside her. "Unk," it remarked.

Gracie's eyes widened. "Gubble! Did it throw you out too?"

"Help." It wasn't clear who or what Gubble was referring to, but Gracie could see he was giving her his broad, toothless grin. "Help." And then, "Help Gracie."

"Oh, Gubble," Gracie said, patting the top of his bald head, "thank you! Thank you so much! Does—does that mean you're coming with me?" She didn't say how very much she hoped he was. The path to Gorebreath was long, crossing through the Less Enchanted Forest and over several hills that eventually led to the Rather Ordinary Woods and the Five Kingdoms, and although the moon was high in the sky, the shadows were extremely dark. A substantial troll would be a comforting companion. And if they did meet with some Deep Magic, at least there would be two of them.

Gubble grunted. "Gubble come too." And he stomped off ahead of Gracie up the winding track.

Chapter Three

"WOW!" the small bat's mouth hung wide open in amazement as he stared at the swirling purple mist. "WOW! Look at *that*!"

"Alf! Close your mouth this minute!" Marlon snapped. "This is serious! That stuff's Evil, that is. Gotta take some action, kiddo."

Alf looked at his uncle in admiration. "What'll we do?"

"*We?*" Marlon frowned. "This ain't no game. This is the big time, kid. You buzz off home. Me, I'm going to have a peek from the other side." And with a flip of his wings, he was gone, leaving his nephew staring indignantly after him.

From beneath the tree a small voice said, "Crones. What is crones, please?"

Alf peered down in surprise. "Excuse me, miss —
were you talking to me?"

Loobly blinked. "Was talking. Yes. What is
crones?"

"They're old, old women," Alf explained. "Live a
long way away. They're . . . they're kind of magic. *Good*
magic." He flew down, landed close to Loobly's head,
and whispered proudly, "I take messages for them!"

Loobly had no way of knowing this wasn't strictly
true, and she looked impressed. Alf had once taken a
message, but only under the critical eyes of his uncle;
Marlon would have been shocked to hear his boast.
Loobly, however, took him at his word. "No take messages," she said firmly. "Take Loobly! Take Loobly
NOW!"

"What?" Alf was suddenly alarmed. It was beginning
to occur to him that there was something odd about
this girl. She didn't sound or look at all like Gracie
Gillypot, who was the only girl he had ever spent much
time with. On the other hand, despite smelling faintly
of cheese, she didn't seem particularly evil.

Loobly glanced in the direction of the purple mist.
It was slowly dissolving, and shadowy figures were
gradually emerging. With a muffled squeak of terror,
she slid in between the trees; Truda Hangnail stood

revealed, her eyes gleaming and her long green tongue flickering as she tasted the night air.

"There's something strange hereabouts," Truda muttered, turning back into the mist.

A moment later she had dragged Evangeline Droop to her side . . . but it was a very different Evangeline from the tall, imposing figure who had made her authoritative way to the weekly Cauldron Fest on Wadingburn Hill. This Evangeline was old, twisted, and bent; her face was covered in large, purple, whiskery warts, and her eyes were blank and expressionless.

"Tell me!" Truda hissed, and she shook Evangeline until her teeth rattled in her head. "I heard you— I heard you calling to someone. Are they in the bushes?"

Evangeline waved a hand. Her mind was still filled with misty confusion and anger at the butcher's boy. "Boils on his nose . . ." she chanted. "Boils on his toes . . ."

Truda shook her again. "TELL ME! Who were you calling?"

"Boils . . ." Evangeline repeated, but she frowned as a different memory floated up from somewhere behind the butcher's boy. "Rats . . . pickled rats . . . where's the pickled rat . . . ?"

With an exasperated snort, Truda dropped Evangeline's arm. "Rats? Rats? I'll give you pickled rats!"

In among the trees, Loobly froze and clutched the rat closer to her skinny chest. "Not Ratty," she mouthed silently. "No hurt Ratty. . . . Please be good to Ratty. . . ."

The fire in the center of the clearing hissed and spat, and Truda swung around to look. A clear blue light sprang up, hovered over the cauldron, then died. Truda jumped, muttering as she turned first one way, then the other, her tongue flickering to and fro until she gave a sudden angry grunt.

"That's a whiff of Trueheart in the air, if I'm not much mistaken—but how come? There are no Truehearts here . . . or are there?" She eyed Evangeline coldly. "You'll tell me who was here sooner or later. I'll see to that!" And she scowled as she moved back toward the center of the clearing.

The purple mist was patchy now, and the witches of Wadingburn stood waiting for her, each of them covered in warts and whiskers and, like Evangeline, with mindless eyes.

Truda smiled. It was not a nice smile. "Now, you witchy women of Wadingburn—you listen to me, and listen well. You're in the power of the Deep Magic, and you'll do what I say."

"Do what you say . . ." the witches of Wadingburn repeated in a monotonous drone.

Truda nodded. "And it's time things changed in this little kingdom of yours. You"—Truda jerked a thumb at her cowering granddaughter—"you invited me to come, and here I'll stay." She gave a high-pitched cackle. "But not in that there poor little shed you call home. No, it's a palace for me. Queen Bluebell's still creaking her way around that palace of hers—but she's got no daughter, and it's a daughter she needs to be queen after she's dead and buried." Truda stopped for a moment. "That's right, isn't it? Only queens can take the throne?"

"Only queens can take the throne," the five witches chanted in unison.

"Well, then!" Truda looked triumphant. "And if there's no daughter, she'll be choosing another fine lady—and I've always had a fancy for silks and satins and a crown. Silks and satins, and servants waiting on me hand and foot." She looked down at her drab and faded black skirts. "A bit of luxury, that's what I want—a bit of luxury, and a nice little kingdom where I can do as I like." Her eyes began to gleam as she envisaged her future. "Queen Truda of Wadingburn, that's what I'm after! And with a handful of Deep Magic here and there, that's what I'll get. Understand?"

The witches swayed from side to side. "Queen Truda of Wadingburn. We understand."

"Excellent! Queen Truda . . . Queen Truda of Wadingburn." The gleam in Truda's eyes shone even brighter as her vision suddenly grew. "And who can tell? Could be I'll be Queen of the Five Kingdoms one of these fine days! But I'll begin right here and now. I'll get the old bag to declare ME her successor, and then—"

She stopped and stared. Something unexpected was happening . . . something so unexpected that she took a sharp step backward. The witches of Wadingburn were growing ever more whiskery, and they were shrinking. What remained of Mrs. Cringe let out an agonized shriek as she reached the size of a largish rat, and Mrs. Vibble and Mrs. Prag went pale beneath their extensive whiskers. Ms. Scurrilous dropped onto all fours and scuttled in an anxious circle, and Evangeline Droop drew herself up to her not-very-full height. Her eyes had completely lost their blank expression, and she was quivering with fury.

"How COULD you?" she squeaked. "Just LOOK at us! I DEMAND to be restored to my correct size AT ONCE!"

Truda Hangnail didn't answer. She was thinking. It was true that her spells misfired from time to time, with surprising results. Those five-legged sheep, for instance. But this? This was different. Very different. Could a Trueheart be involved? The Witches' Handbook (Deep Edition) warned that calling up the power of Deep Magic in the presence of a Trueheart could result in unwanted side effects. . . .

Truda ground her teeth in fury. If a Trueheart, or anything resembling a Trueheart, was responsible for spoiling her spell, she would make quite certain that he or she never had the chance to do it again. But in the meantime, there were five small and exceedingly whiskery women standing in a row on the grass in front of her, and they were no longer her willing slaves. They looked angry. Very angry . . . and Truda decided to consider the matter of the Trueheart later.

"Now, now, now, ladies," she said in a conciliatory tone. "Ladies — don't go fretting yourselves. I do have a plan. . . ."

"It had better be a good one!" squeaked Mrs. Prag,

and Mrs. Vibble and Ms. Scurrilous shrilled their agreement.

"It's very simple," Truda promised. "You help me, and I help you—"

She stopped midsentence. The animal draped around her neck had suddenly raised its head and hissed in her ear.

"*What?*" Truda's face darkened as she glared into the shadows, where the trembling Loobly was hidden. "A sneeze, Malice? WHO sneezed?"

Malice, created by Truda from snake, rat, and weasel, complete with the very nastiest characteristics of all three, whispered again. Puffs of purple smoke shot from Truda's nostrils. "Just you wait here," she told the witches, and she strode toward the trees.

"*Run!*" Alf fluttered wildly under Loobly's nose. "RUN!"

Loobly ran.

Chapter Four

Buckleup Brandersby, Master-in-Charge of the Happy Times Orphanage ("Orphans of Any Age speedily collected from anywhere in the Five Kingdoms and kept in a Caring and Supportive Environment in buildings located on the Healthiest Gravel Soil near the Ancient Town of Wadingburn"), was muttering darkly to himself. He'd had his doubts about sending Loobly Higgins out on work experience right from the start. If he'd had his way, Loobly would have stayed safely in the orphanage washhouse where she belonged, but the ladies on the committee had decided otherwise.

"It is *so* important that a child like Loobly has a fair chance," Mrs. Withery had insisted. "We know she's not exactly one of us. But she's a dear little soul. And Evangeline Droop IS her aunt."

"Excuse me, missus, but she's not really." Buckleup Brandersby shook his large and heavy head. "She only calls her Auntie for politeness, if you don't mind my mentioning it. Met on a orphanage open-house day; seems they took to each other, talking about black cats and frogs and rats and the like. That's all it was. Miss Droop never sends the girl so much as a birthday card—not that we knows when her birthday is, of course, seeing as she was left on the doorstep in an egg basket with no note nor nothing."

"Nevertheless, there is a connection." Mrs. Withery's tone was sharp. She suspected the Master-in-Charge was concerned for himself rather than for Loobly's welfare. As long as an orphan was safely under his roof, he earned himself a silver shilling a week and a loaf of bread. Orphans who vanished meant losing both, and judging from the extreme rotundity of Buckleup's stomach, any reduction in sandwiches would be regarded by him as a serious matter.

"And you never know," Mrs. Withery went on, "little Loobly could have a feeling for witchcraft. Just imagine"—her eyes grew wide with a vision— "the witches of Wadingburn might offer her an apprenticeship!"

Buckleup did his best not to sniff. He had no time

for witches, especially witches who declined to contribute to the Happy Times Orphanage Fund. His last appeal ("Make an Orphan's Day by Providing the Funds to buy Him—or Her—a Woolly Vest") had met with nothing more than this offer of work experience, with the proviso that the orphan chosen was to be obedient, female, and not afraid of frogs, rats, or spiders.

"So it's decided, then?" Mrs. Withery had looked around at the other members of the committee. "Loobly Higgins will be sent to spend a week with the witches? Returning home every night, of course."

The vote had been passed, with Buckleup's the only negative voice.

And now Loobly was missing. For the past five days, she had turned up more or less at the right time, but this was her last day—and she wasn't back. Buckleup looked at his clock, and his face darkened ominously. Half-past midnight. She'd been given an extension so that she could accompany the witches to their weekly Cauldron Fest, but it had been on the strict understanding that she was to be back at the orphanage by ten at the latest. Buckleup growled and stomped off to let the dogs out.

Chapter Five

Loobly, stumbling and scrambling in and out of the trees, her breath catching in her throat, gradually became aware of a voice in her ear. A voice that wasn't Alf's. "Don't *run*, kiddo—*climb!*" it insisted. "Swing a left, and go *up!*"

Too scared to do anything except blindly obey, Loobly turned left and found her way barred by an ancient oak tree. Tucking Ratty into a pocket of her dress, she began to climb, still urged on by the voice.

"Keep going, kid! There's a fork coming up—keep right! Good—now up again!"

Her arms aching, Loobly did as she was told.

It wasn't until she began to see the stars twinkling between the branches above her that the voice finally said, "OK. Take a break, kiddo. You deserve it."

From far down below came the sound of another voice. Truda was hissing angrily as a twist of thorny blackberry bush caught at her ankle, and as she tried to disentangle herself, another twist caught her other foot. Furious, she pulled a handful of bone dust from her bag and scattered it with a mumbled spell. At once the tangle of thorns dissolved away into a steaming purple puddle, and Truda stepped free, slapping at the creature around her neck as she did so.

"A waste of dragon's bone," she croaked. "Sneeze, indeed! If you can't do better than that, Malice, I'll see you made into gloves!"

Malice didn't answer. He knew someone totally lacking in evil had been close; he could sense it in the air, but now there was no sign. No sign at all. And he disliked being slapped and threatened. He closed his eyes firmly and put himself to sleep.

Truda felt him fading and considered hurling him into the darkness, but on second thought she decided against it. He had his uses, even if he did fall asleep at the most inconvenient moments. "Should have added dog for obedience when I made him," she muttered. Malice smiled sourly in the midst of his dreams, and Truda peered this way and that into the darkness.

"No scent . . . Where's that dratted Trueheart gone?" Her green tongue flickered. There were bats nearby, but that wasn't in any way unusual, and there was a strong odor of rat, but that too was of no interest to her. Could Malice have been wrong? Was it really a Trueheart who had sneezed? Something or someone had twisted her spell, but it seemed that whatever it was had vanished. Truda shook her head and turned to go back to the clearing. Pushing her way between the bushes and trees she saw that the moon had come out from behind the clouds, and in its light the cauldron shone silver . . . and solitary. Of the witches of Wadingburn, there was no sign.

Truda cursed under her breath. It seemed as if even Mrs. Cringe had deserted her, but as she stormed her way out from the trees, she heard a small squeak, and the diminutive figure of her elderly granddaughter scuttled toward her.

"Grandma! Where were you? Can't you hear the dogs?"

Truda lifted her head and listened. The sound of distant barking floated up from the bottom of Wadingburn Hill.

"That's hounds," Mrs. Cringe whimpered. "They're

on someone's trail. What if they come up here? Snap us up in a whisker, they will—you've got to do something! Call up that magic of yours—at least call it up if it'll do any good."

The icy glare that Truda turned on her granddaughter made the miniature witch quail.

"Not that I doubt you," she said hastily. "But there's been a bit too much shrinkage going on, if you ask me. When do we get to grow—" She stopped mid-sentence. The barking was getting closer, and Mrs. Cringe clutched at her grandmother's skirts. "DO SOMETHING!" she wailed, and as she spoke, the four remaining witches popped out of the surrounding undergrowth like so many rabbits, twittering with fear.

Truda glanced around. If a pack of dogs arrived, there was not going to be time for pleasant chitchat before they found what they might well consider a collection of edible rodents. "Here!" she ordered, and bending down, she swept up Mrs. Cringe, Mrs. Vibble, and Ms. Scurrilous and deposited them in the cauldron. Another swoop, and Evangeline and Mrs. Prag joined the others in the extreme discomfort of a large metal cooking pot that was still unpleasantly warm and damp.

Truda was only just in time; as she straightened up, the first of the dogs came leaping toward her.

Up in the topmost branches of the oak tree, Loobly gave an anguished squeak. The moon was full and very bright, and she could see the animals circling around the cauldron. She could also make out the stout and panting figure of Buckleup Brandersby as he toiled his way up the hill.

"Keep cool, kiddo. You're doing good."

Loobly wobbled and had to clutch at a branch to save herself. "Please—who *is* you?"

"That's Uncle Marlon!" Alf sounded shocked as he fluttered beside her. "*Everyone* knows him."

"Oh." Loobly turned wide eyes on the older bat and studied him. Marlon shifted along his twig into the moonlight and winked at her. "No worries, kiddo. Soon have you safe and—"

A crescendo of barking interrupted him, and, looking down, Loobly took a sharp breath. The lead dog had picked up her trail and was heading straight toward her tree, the others behind him. Buckleup was leaning on the cauldron, his face streaming with sweat, and it was obvious that he was quite extraordinarily angry.

"Runaway norphan, miss." His voice carried clearly as he spoke to Truda. "Dogs know what they're doing, though. Snarler'll have her before the night's over — and WON'T I make her sorry!"

Truda Hangnail breathed in his frustration and fury with an ecstatic smile. "What *fun*," she hissed, then leaned toward him. "Maybe I could—"

"WO-O-O-O-O-O-O-O-O-OWWWW!" The piercing howl drowned out her words, and a ferocious grin spread over Buckleup's greasy face.

"Snarler's got her," he said triumphantly. "Snarler's got her!"

Chapter Six

Gracie and Gubble were making steady progress. Gubble had never been a fast walker; a short, stout troll is not built for speed. He had other skills, however; whenever the undergrowth threatened to be too thick for Gracie to push through, he simply shut his eyes and continued his progress. In this way he and Gracie were able to take several shortcuts, leaving a trail of flattened grass and battered bushes behind them. Gracie was wishing she had had time to put on something more substantial than her bedroom slippers, which were already extremely damp; fortunately her bathrobe was thick flannel, and kept the rest of her comfortably warm. Slipping her hands into her pockets, she was pleasantly surprised to find a package of cookies, which she decided to keep for breakfast. *And we're sure to find some berries,* she told herself, *and there are plenty of streams along the way.*

"Berries," Gubble announced as if he had read her thoughts, pointing with a thick, stubby finger at a small, low-growing bush. Gracie stooped and picked a handful, while Gubble helped himself from the other side. "Good," he said approvingly, and only when there were no berries left did he stomp off once more along the narrow path. Gracie followed him, eating as she went. She was pleased to find that the berries tasted of chocolate cake; she had eaten them before and knew that they had a delightful habit of tasting exactly like her favorite foods. The first time she had taken the journey to the House of the Ancient Crones, she had been guided by Marlon, and he had found her the same kind of berries to eat—but until that time Gracie had eaten only potato peelings or porridge skin, and the glories of the berries had almost passed her by. Having been adopted by the crones, she was now aware that her lost and not-at-all-lamented stepfather had fed her a very limited diet; she had had plenty of time and opportunity to experiment with all kinds of delicious treats, but chocolate cake remained her favorite. Gubble, grunting happily, had obviously found

something equally to his taste, and he stomped his way among thistles and stinging nettles with enthusiasm.

"I wonder what we'll find in Gorebreath," Gracie said as she avoided a broken thistle that was doing its best to retaliate. "And I wonder what we can do to help." She sighed. "The House did seem very certain we needed to go at once, so it must really be urgent. I do hope nothing's wrong at the palace."

"Unk." Gubble waved an arm and turned to give Gracie a wide smile. "Marcus?"

A faint wave of pink, hidden by the night, swept across Gracie's face. "Erm . . . yes. I suppose I was wondering about him. Just a little bit, you understand."

"Prince." Gubble waved the other arm. "Prince Marcus. Unk."

Gracie, rightly interpreting this as meaning that Gubble thought of Prince Marcus as his friend, said hopefully, "Do you think maybe we should go to the palace first?"

Gubble shook his head, and Gracie suppressed a small sigh. She knew he was right; they were far more likely to pick up news and gossip in the marketplace. Prince Marcus of Gorebreath was the only one in the palace who went out to look for adventures in the world beyond the Five Kingdoms. The rest of his

family concentrated on being royal; they undertook the necessary state visits, openings of festivals, kissing of babies, and waving to peasants with an admirable devotion to duty and no imagination whatsoever. There were, of course, also a number of social occasions involving princesses from Dreghorn or Wadingburn, Niven's Knowe or Cockenzie Rood, but Gracie preferred not to think about that particular aspect of Marcus's life. She was especially not thinking about the Declaration Ball in Wadingburn and Queen Bluebell's eightieth-birthday party.

"I mean," she said to herself as she and Gubble panted up a steep, gorse-covered hill, "why ever would they have thought of asking me? It's not as if I was a princess or anything like that. Marcus and I were just . . . just companions in an adventure. That's all." She squinted up at a small star twinkling overhead and suddenly felt more cheerful. "But if this turns out to be another adventure, I suppose he might be interested. In fact, I probably ought to tell him about it. After all, adventures are what he likes best." She smiled up at the star and jumped over a small stream. "Why don't I find out what's going on, and then tell Marcus?" And Gracie Gillypot positively skipped for the next few miles, even though her bedroom slippers were now soaked through.

Chapter Seven

Buckleup Brandersby was wrong. Snarler had run straight into the still-steaming mire where Truda had destroyed the blackberry bushes, and his feet were on fire. Several other dogs skidded after him, and their howls mixed with his in a cacophony of agony. Together they limped back to their master, and the smile was wiped from Buckleup's face.

He lurched toward them, staring angrily. "What's this?" Even by moonlight the large blisters and boils that had sprung up on Snarler's paws could be seen to have a purplish glow, and Buckleup's mean little eyes blinked. "By my grandmother's bunions," he muttered to himself, and took a quick step backward. "I've not seen the likes of that since Deep Magic was banned—but Deep Magic is what that is, sure as hens are chickens."

Far up above, at the top of the tree, Loobly's eyes filled with tears. "Poorly doggies," she whispered. "Bad badness . . . no hurt doggies. Please be good to doggies."

Down on the ground, Truda had no intention whatsoever of being good to anyone, human or animal. Her brain was working overtime. She had recognized a possible ally in Buckleup Brandersby — cruelty and unpleasantness hung about him like a murky fog — but could he be bent to her will? She sidled nearer and inspected Snarler and his companions as they rolled on their backs, whimpering pathetically. There was nothing she could do to make their paws more comfortable — Truda's repertory of spells had never included any kind of remedy or antidote — but it might be to her advantage if she put them out of their misery by turning them into toads.

"Or vipers," she said, thinking aloud.

Buckleup gave her a considering look. At first he had taken her for one of the witches of Wadingburn, but he had met Evangeline and her cronies from time to time, and this was a witch of a very different type. Evangeline would have had cold cream and sympathy all over the dogs by now, disregarding their drooling jaws and sharpened teeth. This witch had

shown nothing but a cool curiosity. "What's that about vipers?" he asked suspiciously.

"No legs," Truda explained, and pointed to the dogs.

"Eh?" Buckleup scratched his balding head.

Truda decided to take a risk. "It's an ordinary sort of spell. Dog. *Whoosh!* Viper. Vipers can come in very handy."

The wailing of the dogs was beginning to get on Buckleup's nerves. Any feeling he had for them was entirely connected with how useful they could be. Snarler had brought down many an escaped orphan and was therefore a Good Thing, but Snarler unable to walk, let alone run, was a liability. "I could use a python or two," he remarked.

Truda nodded briskly and fished in her pocket for her bag of bones. Pulling it out, she tossed a handful over the squirming dogs. A shower of hissing sparks flew up in the air, turned bright blue, and floated gently down. Snarler and his companions leaped to their completely healed feet, let out a couple of surprised yelps, and hurled themselves at Truda and Buckleup in an ecstasy of gratitude, their tails wagging madly.

"DOWN!" Buckleup roared, and as the dogs obeyed, he turned to Truda.

She was trembling with suppressed rage. "Trueheart!" she hissed.

"What's that?" Buckleup pushed Snarler away as the dog tried to lick his hand. "What's a Trueheart? And where's my snake?"

Truda did her best to look as if she were in control of the situation. "You've got your dogs back, haven't you?"

Buckleup folded his arms. "Just a minute. You said you were going to give me a python. I don't say as I'm not grateful that Snarler's back on his pins, but a snake's a snake, and a deal's a deal." He stroked his bristly chin thoughtfully. "Good at tracking, are they? I've got a missing norphan, and I need to catch her pronto."

"Use your dogs," Truda snapped. She was feeling decidedly unwell. She was used to the occasional malfunction in her Deep Magic spells, as there was no quality control over dragon's bone, but it seemed that here in the Five Kingdoms, nothing she did turned out as she had expected. She wanted to practice a little serious nastiness without this large, foolish man glaring at her.

Buckleup grunted angrily but whistled his dogs back around him. "I'll be waiting for that snake," he

growled. "Like I say—a deal's a deal. And if you happen to see a skinny little wretch of a norphan trailing along the road, tell her I'll have her on toast for breakfast." He yawned and gave a last look around. "Could be she's slipped back to the orphanage after all. She has no more brain than a parsnip, so she could have gotten lost—but if she's not there, I'll be after her first thing tomorrow!" And he stormed away down the hill, the dogs gamboling happily at his heels.

"Yoo-hoo! Truda!"

The plaintive cry echoing faintly from the depths of the cauldron made Truda start. Slowly she walked toward the cauldron and peered in. The five witches were squashed together at the bottom, looking cross, disheveled and damp around the feet. Truda leaned on the metal rim and stared thoughtfully down at them. It had never occurred to her before that moment that the ability to shrink small and grow tall could be extremely useful. The singularly unexpected shrinking of the witches of Wadingburn could, perhaps, be turned to her advantage after all.

"Now, listen," she began. "I saved you from those dogs, so you owe me. Isn't that right?"

Insofar as they were able, the witches nodded,

Mrs. Prag trying her best to avoid sticking her elbow in Evangeline's eye.

"Good," Truda went on, "and don't you go forgetting it. Like I said, I've got plans, and having a few little creatures to do a bit of spying could come in handy. You can go scuttling and creeping and listening, and that's what I want. There's things I need to know, and you can find out. What's the old bag thinking? What's she planning? What's this Declaration? Has she found anyone to be queen after her?" She let out a high-pitched cackle. "It's to be a Declaration Ball, you say. . . . Well, if I have my way, it'll be to declare Truda Hangnail as Queen of Wadingburn!"

Evangeline let out a tiny protesting squeak, and Truda glared at her.

"Don't you go trying to trick me! I'll call that fool and his dogs if you do . . . or do you want to be a pipsqueak forever and ever?"

There was a pause as the five witches paled beneath their whiskers.

"So, you'll be doing as I say." Truda folded her arms.

There was an immediate chorus of enthusiastic agreement from inside the cauldron.

Truda nodded. "That's what I like to hear," she said, and she tipped the heavy metal pot onto its side.

There was a flurrying and a scurrying as the contents disentangled themselves, and Evangeline Droop pulled herself to her total height of some ten inches. "As the Grand High Witch of Wadingburn, I'm taking it upon myself to speak for my fellow witches," she announced. "I'd like—"

"Speak for yourself, dearie," Mrs. Cringe interrupted. "I'm sticking with Grandma. Seems to me that she's the one who says what's what just now, not you."

Evangeline bit her lip but did her best to continue. "We'll do as Mrs. Hangnail asks, but in return I'd like a solemn oath that once she's achieved her aims, she'll leave us in peace."

"But she'll be Queen of Wadingburn, ducky!" Mrs. Cringe gave Evangeline a triumphant leer. "So *you* won't be needed, far as I can see. We'll be dancing to *your* tune then, won't we, Grandma? And if Grandma's queen, that makes me a princess—so you'll be lucky if I send you to fetch my shoes!"

Truda looked down at her whiskery granddaughter. While approving her sentiments, she had noticed that Mrs. Prag, Mrs. Vibble, and Ms. Scurrilous had moved to stand close to their former leader, and division could be dangerous. She smiled coldly at Evangeline. "I'm

sure there'll be no need to be troubling you again," she
said, without meaning a word.

"Can't I stay with you, Grandma?" Mrs. Cringe put
a hopeful hand on her relative's boot. "They say that
palace is infested with rats, and I never could abide
their horrible, scaly tails. Let me stay with you! I'll be
no trouble."

Truda's eyes flashed as she bent down. "Who's going
to keep an eye on that fancy Grand High Witch if you
aren't there?" she hissed. "She's as Shallow as they
come. And you'll be seeing me soon enough—don't
you worry!"

Mrs. Cringe perked up immediately. Spying on
her so-called friends was always a pleasure, and the
thought of being able to tell tales about Evangeline
made her quiver with excitement. "Of course," she
whispered hoarsely. "Won't let her out of my sight!"

"That's it." Truda nodded. She watched the five
little cloaked figures bob away down the moonlit path
and considered her plans. "So the palace is infested
with rats, is it? I'll remember that. Where there are
rats, there are tunnels and holes and secret ways.
But for now there's that Trueheart to deal with." She
turned to the cauldron. Tossing in a handful of bone,

she began to mutter. A moment later, a thin, purplish snake with glittering black eyes slid over the rim, and Truda rubbed her skinny hands together. "See that, Malice?" she crowed. "Nothing wrong with *my* spells." She pointed at the snake. "Find the Trueheart. Go!"

But Loobly was gone. As soon as Buckleup Brandersby and his dogs had tramped away, Marlon had persuaded her to slip down from the tree and follow him on a zigzag journey down the hill. Loobly had done as she was told without complaint, even when he'd insisted she paddle across a freezing stream not just once but several times.

"No smell in water, kiddo," he said. "It'll keep whatever's after you off the scent."

"But the dogs went the other way," Alf pointed out.

"There's things worse than dogs," Marlon told him severely, and as they flitted on through the wavering moonlight, Alf saw with some astonishment that they were heading toward the outskirts of Wadingburn village.

"Where are we going, Uncle Marlon?" he asked.

"To see crones." Loobly's voice was small but definitive.

Marlon did a backflip, landed on a twig, and gave

Loobly what Alf thought of as Uncle Marlon's Serious
Stare. "Listen, kiddo," he said, "do you want to help
your auntie?"

Loobly nodded.

"Then we don't go to the crones," Marlon told her.
"'Scuse me saying so, but you wouldn't travel fast. We
need to play close, and we need to play clever. Right?"
He did not add that he thought it highly unlikely
that Loobly would ever make it to the House of the
Ancient Crones before being found either by Buckleup
Brandersby's dogs or by Truda Hangnail. He was also
aware that he could reach the crones much faster if he
was unimpeded.

"Right," Loobly echoed, but her small, grimy face
was screwed up in confusion.

"We'll put you where they'll never think of looking,
kiddo." Marlon winked at her. "Check this out. Where
d'you hide a big black cat?"

Alf did a double spin and squeaked, "In a big black
cellar!"

Marlon shook his head. "Good, Alfie boy, but not
good enough. Get the dogs out — they'd find it right
off. Nah — you put your big black cat in the middle of
a dozen big black cats." He waved a wing at Loobly.
"Small, skinny — 'scuse me, kiddo, but facts are

facts — we'll put you in the palace kitchen. There's at least a dozen small, skinny kitchen maids — you'll vanish. And that Truda dame? Last place she'll look for you."

"Queenly palace?" Loobly looked more confused than ever as she pushed her hair out of her eyes. "But —"

"But me no buts," Marlon said grandly. "You'll do fine, kid. And once you're safely stashed, I'll tell the crones what's what, and we'll know how to get your auntie fixed up. OK?"

Loobly bit her lip, then nodded. "Please fix Auntie, Mr. Bat."

"Wilco. Now, time to fly!" And Marlon set off with Alf flapping close behind him. Loobly ran to keep up.

Chapter Eight

If Marlon had been able to hear a conversation taking place early the following morning, he would have been even more delighted with his decision. Buckleup Brandersby, finding that Loobly had not returned to the orphanage, had gotten up at the crack of dawn with the firm intention of finding her. After cheering himself up by canceling breakfast for every orphan in the orphanage, he had whistled for the dogs and set off once more for Wadingburn Hill. There he found Truda Hangnail, who had spent what remained of the night practicing her spells and concocting nasty-looking potions in the cauldron. She was feeling much better; she had perfected the art of shrinking and growing to the point where she could reduce herself to the size of a rat with the snap of a finger, and she had almost managed to convince herself that the shrinking of the Wadingburn witches was all her own work. Several bald wood pigeons, a squirrel with two tails, and a collection of poisonous biting beetles demonstrated that she had not lost her Deep Magic touch. She was not pleased to see Buckleup; she had decided that although he was wicked and cruel, he was also dull.

"What do you want?" she asked him.

Buckleup didn't answer. He was holding an old and well-worn sock out to the dogs. "Find Loobly!" he commanded. The dogs began to circle the clearing, sniffing as they went.

Truda watched them sourly. "Are you looking for the witches?"

Buckleup shook his head. "Told you. A norphan. Loobly Higgins. Spindly little thing. She was here for certain; Snarler was hot on her trail last night. She went with the witches to Cauldron Fest, but she never came back."

Truda's voice suddenly sharpened. "I don't suppose she had anything to do with that one calling herself the Grand High Witch? Evangeline Droop? She called to someone, and I'd say that someone could have been hiding in those bushes. Malice"—she indicated the

drooping furry creature hanging around her neck—
"heard a sneeze."

Hearing his name, Malice yawned, stretched, and
raised his head to whisper in her ear.

"What?" Truda's eyebrows rose. "She said *what*?"

Malice whispered again, and Buckleup leaned forward to try to catch what he was saying.

"The crones—what's that? What's he talking about?
What's that about the crones?"

Truda was looking thoughtful and also angry. "Her.
Evangeline. Malice"—she gave the animal a vicious
slap—"Malice says she was telling your Loobly to find
the Ancient Crones . . . so I'd say that's where she's
gone. And what I'd like to know is why he didn't think
to mention it before!"

Buckleup stared at Malice, and Malice leered back.

"The crones, eh?" Buckleup stroked his chin.
"They're a funny lot. Best not messed with, by all
accounts."

"Rubbish!" Truda snapped. "You've got dogs,
haven't you? From what my granddaughter tells me,
those crones live right on the other side of the Five
Kingdoms. She can't fly, can she, this Loobly? You'd
catch her long before she got to Gorebreath."

Buckleup Brandersby, unaware that Truda had her own reasons for wanting Loobly caught but sensing her urgency, brightened. "You're right, missus. I'll be on my way." He gave Truda an evil wink. "And I'll make sure she never thinks to run away again once I've got her safely back in that there washhouse. Don't you go worrying yourself about that!" And he called to his dogs and set off briskly.

As Truda watched him go, she considered what she'd discovered. An orphan named Loobly Higgins had been hiding when she had cast her Deep Magic. There had been the smell of Trueheart in the air at the time . . . so surely it was only reasonable to assume that the orphan was a Trueheart and therefore responsible for the alteration of the spells. Truda sucked angrily at a tooth. Her power over the witches had been seriously undermined, and she was now obliged to rule them by fear; only Mrs. Cringe could be entirely trusted. If Truda was to succeed in her plan to become Queen of Wadingburn, there was no doubt that the Trueheart orphan must be kept well out of her way.

"Once she's back in that orphanage, she'd better not get out again," Truda told herself, but remembering the expression on Buckleup Brandersby's face, she relaxed. It was unlikely that Loobly would ever see the light of day again once she was caught. "So what next?" She folded her arms and surveyed the kingdom stretched out below. "Maybe it's time to see what those little witchy ladies are up to. I'll shrink myself and spy on my spies . . . and see the palace for myself." The idea of sneaking up on the witches of Wadingburn tickled Truda, and she cackled again. In the distance, Buckleup Brandersby felt the hairs on the back of his neck tingle uncomfortably, and Snarler lifted up his head and howled.

Chapter Nine

As the morning sun lit the top of the looms, the Ancient One came stomping into room seventeen, her one bright blue eye glaring fiercely. She waved a piece of paper scrawled on in violet ink under the Oldest's nose. "Elsie! Gracie's gone! I've just found a ridiculous note written by that dratted pen on the kitchen door. It says she's gone to save the Five Kingdoms. When did you last see her?"

Elsie quailed. "She brought me some tea around midnight," she said. "She mentioned something about the quill pen writing on her walls, and then she disappeared. I thought she'd gone back to bed. I wasn't really listening to her; I was so worried about the stain on the web. It's Deep Magic, Edna—there's no doubt about it!"

"Exactly," the Ancient One said drily. "It is indeed

Deep Magic, and it seems to me that you've allowed Gracie to walk out into the thick of it."

Elsie burst into a noisy fit of crying. "Oh, I'm sorry, Edna—I really am! But the House was rumbling this way and that all night, and what with that and the web, I never thought for a minute she'd do anything so amazingly brave."

The Ancient One looked marginally less angry. "Brave, or just plain silly," she remarked. "But I didn't know the House was up to its tricks as well." She sighed. "That's the trouble with a Trueheart House. It doesn't believe in being cautious when it comes to defeating evil."

"Has anyone seen Gubble?" Val, the Youngest, was standing in the doorway yawning. She lived outside the House with her brother, Professor Scallio, but arrived early each morning to take up her duties, which included making breakfast. "His cupboard was empty when I got here, and even when I called him for his boiled egg, he didn't appear. And Gracie seems to have vanished as well—"

"Oh, Val!" Elsie pointed at the purple stain on the silver web. "Look! There's Deep Magic somewhere about, and Gracie's gone off to find it, and she might be getting herself into dreadful trouble!"

"That's a worry." Val seated herself at the loom as Elsie got up. "But do you know what? I'd say Gubble's gone with her. He's devoted to Gracie — and I've never known him to miss a boiled egg before."

Edna's blue eye brightened. "If she's got Gubble with her, I won't worry quite so much. We'll just have to wait and see what happens."

"I could go after them," Elsie suggested, but the Ancient One shook her head.

"Certainly not," she said firmly. "With luck, the two of them'll be back before long, safe and sound. And we've got the Newest and all her tantrums to cope with, and that length of blue velvet needs to be finished. Princess Nina-Rose won't have a dress for Queen Bluebell's birthday party if it's not finished today." She paused to snort derisively. "Declaration Ball, indeed! Whom do you think she's chosen to be queen after her? None of those Five Kingdoms' princesses can hold a candle to our Gracie, but presumably the queen's chosen one of them, seeing as her own daughter's not around. Clever way to announce it, mind you."

The two other crones nodded, and while Elsie went to get her breakfast, Val continued the weaving of the silver web. Edna walked to the window and looked out. It seemed as if she had quieted her companions' fears for the moment, but she hadn't convinced herself. The purple stain was spreading, and even the most solid and robust of trolls would be little protection if Gracie found herself in the midst of seriously Deep Magic.

But she is *a Trueheart,* the Ancient One thought. *And sensible with it. She'll be all right . . . I hope.*

Chapter Ten

In the Royal State Room of Wadingburn Palace, Prince Vincent was blissfully happy. It was State Visit Friday, and he was standing in for his grandmother, Queen Bluebell the Twenty-eighth, who had declared that she was going to arrive later. She had a terrible cold, and Vincent was secretly hoping she might not get up at all. Normally firmly suppressed by his illustrious grandmother, he was making the most of his opportunity as he worked his way around the crowded room.

"Did I tell you about the different kinds of cake we're having at Grandmother's Declaration Ball tomorrow?" he asked Queen Kesta of Dreghorn.

Queen Kesta, who had already heard about the soups, the fish, the pies, and the ice creams, stifled a yawn. "No, dear," she said as politely as she could. "Do tell me."

Prince Vincent beamed at her, but he had hardly finished describing the first of the eight different varieties of cake before Queen Kesta's eyes closed. The prince, certain she was imagining the glories of rose-petal cream, continued unabashed.

Princess Nina-Rose, Queen Kesta's oldest daughter, had managed to escape from Vincent somewhere between the pies and the ice cream, but having been bored beyond belief, she was feeling decidedly contrary. She was sitting on a window seat, gazing out the window, while behind her, Prince Arioso, heir to the kingdom of Gorebreath, stood on one leg, looking forlorn.

"But *why* won't you promise me the first dance?" he asked plaintively. "You said you would the other day."

Nina-Rose shrugged a shoulder and went on looking out the window.

Marcus, Arioso's twin brother, squashed a strong desire to box her ears. Marcus had little time for princesses who spent their time fluttering fans, changing their minds, and worrying about frilly dresses. He also disliked the fact that his brother, older by exactly ten minutes, looked like a lost puppy whenever he was near Nina-Rose. He sighed, squinted up at the ballroom clock, and was depressed to discover that it was only three minutes since he'd last looked. State visits were supposed to last at least an hour, and so far they had managed only a quarter of the allotted time— although fifteen minutes of Prince Vincent had made it feel like several days already. "If you don't feel like talking, I'm sure Vincent wouldn't mind if Arry and I left a bit early," he said hopefully.

Nina-Rose shrugged the other shoulder, and Arry's face grew even longer. Marcus sighed impatiently and moved toward the door, but Arioso shot him a pleading look.

Rolling his eyes, Marcus sat down again, wondering why his twin brother—so like him to look at—was so completely different in character. Arry was a model of good behavior, never caused trouble, and actually seemed to enjoy royal duties that made Marcus squirm with boredom. Indeed, Marcus would never have come on the visit to Wadingburn Palace if he hadn't been in need of Arry's help; state visits were extremely low on Marcus's list of essential activities, but Arioso adored them and liked Marcus to keep him company. Adventures, however, were something else, and Marcus had in mind a plan to explore the Less Enchanted Forest beyond the borders of the Five Kingdoms . . . a plan that would mean he was away from home overnight. This was something his parents would not allow under any circumstances, so he needed Arry to come down to breakfast twice, once as himself, and then—rather later, and in a terrible hurry—pretending to be Marcus. The two of them were so alike that even King Frank and Queen Mildred couldn't always tell them apart; only Marcus's complete lack of concern about clothes, and a tendency to have his hair sticking up in tufts, distinguished him from Arioso.

Marcus looked at the clock again. Seventeen minutes gone. Nina-Rose was still staring out the window, and Arry was still drooping. All around the room little groups of princesses were giggling and peeping at the princes over the tops of their fans, and sooner or later he'd be forced into conversation with one or another of them. Something had to be done, or he'd go completely mad.

"What if Arry went on a quest?" he asked suddenly. "You know—like the knights of old? Caught a dragon for you, or something like that? Would you dance with him then?"

Arry looked horrified, but Nina-Rose turned around. "I wouldn't like a dragon," she said, wrinkling her nose disdainfully. "It would make too much of a mess. All that nasty fire and trampling about."

Marcus saw a glimmer of hope. "Not a dragon, then. A mermaid? A griffin?"

Nina-Rose gave Arry a sideways look, making sure he got the full benefit of her exceedingly long eyelashes. "Would you really go on a quest for me?"

Aware that Arry was quite likely to say that he would do anything for Nina-Rose just as long as it didn't involve foolishness and danger, Marcus slapped his twin so hard on the back that Arry coughed instead of answering.

"Of course he would," Marcus promised. "He never stops talking about you and how wonderful you are." This was true. "He's always saying he can't wait to prove how much he adores you." This was not true, but Nina-Rose went a delicate shade of pink and smiled at Arry for the first time since he had arrived.

"Oh, Arry *darling*," she breathed. "How amazing of you! As it happens, there *is* something I'd really, really like." She paused to consider the effect she was having on Arry and noticed an apprehensive look in his eyes. Annoyed, she went on, "That is, if you really *are* brave enough. If you aren't, I'm sure Prince Albion of

Cockenzie Rood would fetch it for me. He promised he'd do *anything* if I'd dance with him. . . ."

"WHAT?" Arry sat bolt upright and looked almost warlike. Marcus grinned. This was more like it. "What is it you want?"

Nina-Rose, now enjoying herself hugely, leaned back against the window with a little sigh of pleasure. "Someone told Mother they'd seen a snow-white peacock in Flailing. I'd *love* a feather from a snow-white peacock for my hair. . . ."

"Consider it yours," Arry said firmly, then paused. "At least—"

"At least nothing," Marcus cut in swiftly, jumping to his feet. "Arry'll be off on his quest at once—won't you, Arry?"

"At once?" Arry looked up at the clock. "But we haven't finished our visit—"

"No time to worry about royal etiquette now," Marcus told him. "I'm sure Nina-Rose will forgive you and give Vincent our apologies for leaving early," and he bowed to the princess as he pried Arry to his feet.

Nina-Rose, who had been wondering what else she could ask for, looked disappointed, but she smiled sweetly enough at Arry. "Of course," she said.

"And you'll dance the first dance with me?" Arry

called over his shoulder as his brother frog-marched him toward the door.

"Oh, Arry . . ." Now that he was leaving, Nina-Rose began to feel pangs of remorse. Arry was, after all, incredibly handsome. And rich. And adoring. "I'd absolutely love to dance with you all night long."

"Wowsers!" Arry's smile nearly split his face in two as they left the room. "Did you hear that, Marcus?"

"I did. Now, come on—we've got to get back to Wadingburn so I can get Glee saddled and ready to go."

"And you'll bring me back that peacock feather?" Arry asked anxiously.

Marcus threw up his hands in frustration. "YES!" And he pushed his brother out the palace door and into the coach that was waiting outside.

Arry climbed in, still beaming. "There's nothing like dancing with the girl you love," he declared as he settled into a corner. "Maybe you'll find a beautiful princess to dance with as well, Marcus. I'm sure Princess Marigold always gives you a special kind of smile when she meets you. Mother was saying you'd make a lovely couple." He lowered his voice. "Nina-Rose told me not to tell you, but Marigold's going to ask you for the Last Waltz."

"Me?" Marcus stopped halfway in and halfway out of the coach. "If I dance with anyone—and I'm not saying I will—it'll be with Gracie Gillypot. She's got more sense in her little finger than any of those frilly sisters of Nina-Rose!"

The smile left Arioso's face. "But Marcus—she won't have been invited!"

"WHAT?" Marcus stared at his brother. "What do you mean, she's not invited?"

Arry shrugged. "I know she's a friend of yours, but she's . . . well, she's only an orphan, isn't she?"

Marcus went on staring while he took in what his brother was saying. Then, with a muttered exclamation, he left the coach and shot back into Wadingburn Palace.

He arrived in front of Prince Vincent in a flurry, and grabbed his arm. "Hey!" he demanded. "You can ask Gracie to this ball, can't you?"

Prince Vincent's mind was full of buttercream icing and strawberry jam. His mouth fell open, and he gaped at Marcus. "Gracie?" he asked vaguely.

"You know—Gracie Gillypot. Lives with the Ancient Crones. Saved you from being a frog once, but I don't suppose you care to remember that."

"Oh—er, yes." Vincent first nodded, then shook

his head. "Actually, I don't suppose she *can* be asked, old boy. Not the right sort of person at all, Gracie Gillypot. Don't want to make her feel out of place, and all that." He coughed. "I mean, once you ask one orphan, they'll all be expecting to come, won't they? Even if she is a friend of yours."

Marcus went a furious purple—but before he could utter a word of protest, a booming voice echoed from the doorway. "A friend of Marcus's? Of course she's invited. ATCHOOO!" Queen Bluebell produced an enormous handkerchief embroidered with the royal arms of Wadingburn and blew her nose with the sound of trumpets. "Especially if it's that little girl who lives with the crones. Good girl, full of spirit. Not like some of the young royals around here, and I'm not talking about you, young Marcus!"

Vincent looked at his grandmother in alarm. "You don't mean *me*, do you, Grandmother?"

Queen Bluebell gave him a withering glance. "If the cap fits, then wear it. *Atchooo!*" She swung around on Marcus, her lorgnette perched on the end of her aristocratic nose. "You tell Gracie Gillypot she's to come on my personal invitation, and she's to sit next to me. Vincent, you're a fool. And a snob besides, and if there's one thing I can't abide, it's a snob. Now—out of my way! I need to talk to dear Kesta about something of the *utmost* importance!" And Queen Bluebell the Twenty-eighth thundered across the polished floor to where Queen Kesta was rubbing her eyes and trying to remember where she was.

As Marcus hurried away to the waiting Arry, he saw something small dressed in black whisk quickly under the grandfather clock in the palace front hall.

Weird, he thought. *Almost looked like a tiny person! Must have been a rat. . . . Wonder if Queen Bluebell knows the rats are dressing up these days?* He grinned as he leaped into the coach and slammed the door. *Good thing Vincent didn't see it. He's always moaning about them.* And then he forgot all about it as he urged the coachman to make top speed back to the palace of Gorebreath. Arry, rattling from side to side as the coach flew over the cobbled roads, couldn't help noticing that Marcus whistled happily all the way home.

Chapter Eleven

Evangeline Droop stifled a squeak as she arrived, trembling, under the old wooden clock.

"Told you to be careful." Mrs. Cringe was unsympathetic, despite the fact that it was she who had persuaded Evangeline to creep out and listen from the inadequate protection of the radiator. "Did he see you?"

Evangeline, still trembling, shook her head. "I'm sure he didn't. He was in such a hurry—he jumped straight into the coach and was off."

"Hmph." Mrs. Cringe made a note to report to her grandmother that the Grand High Witch had put their lives in serious danger. "Right, ladies. We need to get into that room and check what the old battle-ax is telling that pal of hers. 'Utmost importance,' eh? Bet that'll be about the Declaration!"

Mrs. Prag sighed wistfully. "I wish there was something to eat. I'm so hungry."

"Aren't we all?" Mrs. Cringe snapped back, and it was true. The five tiny witches had found nothing to eat on their long journey from Wadingburn Hill to the palace gardens. Only the thought of Truda Hangnail's wrath had kept them going—that, and the hope of being restored to their proper selves. They had reached the palace as dawn broke over the hills and had made their way inside, thanks to a forgetful maid who had left the boot-room window wide open. The Virginia creeper that covered the palace walls had proved easy to climb, and the five small spies had arrived in a heap among the boots and shoes piled up and waiting to be cleaned. There was a worrying number of rattraps; fortunately they remained unoccupied, and despite some suspicious scuttling noises that left Mrs. Cringe in a state of extreme nervous agitation, no rats had appeared. This was just as well, as the boot-room door was locked solid, and the witches of Wadingburn had had to wait there until the boot boy came, yawning and stretching, to begin his duties. It wasn't until his departure to beg some bread and jam from the cook that they could go any farther. A terrifying dash along an endless corridor had led them to a swinging baize-covered door, and by all heaving together, they had managed to find themselves in the grand marble hall of Wadingburn Palace.

Two minutes later, royal visitors had begun to arrive, and they had been lucky to find a hiding place beneath the clock, taking care to avoid yet another rattrap. They had stayed there, quivering, until Mrs. Cringe had dared Evangeline to make a dash for the radiator, but the gurgling of the ancient water pipes had effectively drowned out most of the conversation from the room beyond. Only the echoing boom of Queen Bluebell's voice could be heard clearly from under the clock.

"There's one thing I noticed," Evangeline said as she recovered her breath. "There are bookcases all around the walls, and there's a gap underneath the bottom shelf. If we slide under at this end, we could creep around the room . . . apart from where there are doors, of course."

Mrs. Cringe, who liked to have the best ideas herself, sniffed. "How do we know there isn't something in the way?"

"We don't." Ms. Scurrilous was getting tired of Mrs. Cringe. "But you said we should try to find out what's going on, and speaking for myself and, I am sure, others of our number, I do *not* wish to be rodent-size for the rest of my life."

"Hear, hear!" Mrs. Prag and Mrs. Vibble nodded, and Evangeline patted Ms. Scurrilous on the back.

"Hmph." Mrs. Cringe, outnumbered, changed her mind. "I was about to say the same myself. Let's get going, then." She eyed the distance between the clock and the bookcase, hesitated, and went on, "Perhaps we should let our leader go first." And she nudged Evangeline.

Evangeline peered out, saw that the coast was clear, and ran. Seeing her disappear safely behind a fretted wooden overhang, Ms. Scurrilous followed, and a moment later all five were creeping up the side of the Royal State Room.

"Kesta, my dear friend," Queen Bluebell boomed, making Evangeline jump. "SUCH a problem! Have you *any* suggestions? I've been racking my brain for months and months, and it's my birthday tomorrow — and *something* has to be done! How can I declare that I've chosen an heir when I've no idea whom to choose?"

Queen Kesta cleared her throat. "I'm sure you don't

need to worry just yet, Bluebell dear. Your mother was at least a hundred and thirty-five when she left us for . . . er . . . the great throne room in the sky."

One of Queen Bluebell's exceptionally large feet began to twitch. "Now, now, Kesta. That is *not* helpful. It's in the Rules of Wadingburn Kingdom: 'The name of the heir apparent must be declared on the occasion of the current ruler's eightieth birthday, and once declared, that name shall not be altered.' All I need is a sensible girl to take over the kingdom—but can I find one? No. And as far as relations go, there's only Vincent." There was the sound of a large and gusty sigh. "We've never had kings in Wadingburn, and I don't intend for us to start now."

Queen Kesta gave a small cough. "Erm . . . I don't like to bring up an unhappy memory, but there's no news of your . . . your daughter?"

There was a second sigh, even larger than the first. "Kesta, my dear, you have the mind of a cuckoo. If there were, do you think I'd be worrying like this?"

"I'm sorry, Bluebell, but it was you who asked if I had any ideas." Queen Kesta was clearly offended. "I was only trying to help."

"My dear friend—forgive me." The large feet stomped across the floor, and the witches guessed, quite correctly, that Queen Kesta was being enveloped in an apologetic hug. "It's all so difficult. *You've* got plenty of well-behaved, docile girls. I had only one girl, and she was trouble from the day she was born. Never did what she was told, never wanted to be a queen, and hasn't been heard of since the day she climbed out of the tower window to run away with the kitchen boy." Queen Bluebell's snort made the windows rattle. "Nice enough boy, Clovis, but no more brain than my grand piano. The whole thing was quite ridiculous! Broad daylight, and the front door wide open, but she has to climb down a rope made of sheets. Fourteen of my best satin sheets, completely ruined. And not a word for seventeen years. Not even a birthday card. Nothing except for that silly young Vincent dumped on my doorstep with his name on a label around his neck and one of Bella's diamond-buckled shoes to show where he came from. Typical Bella! Refuses to be queen, and then produces a boy—the first in twenty-eight genera- tions. But you know all about that, Kesta—I've bored you with the story a hundred times."

There was the sort of polite "Um" that meant her listener had indeed heard the story a good many times but wished to suggest that she had never been bored.

Bluebell took no notice and went on, "Of course,

I still send out search parties, but there isn't a sign of her. I've offered endless rewards, but I've had to accept it: she's gone, and she's not coming back. She'd have been Queen Bluebell the Twenty-ninth, and I can't say that she'd have been any good at it, but at least she'd have had the royal blood in her veins."

"So . . . this Declaration Ball." Queen Kesta was thinking out loud. "Are you hoping Bella will come to it? Or are you looking for a princess who can take her place? Or a wife for Vincent?"

"Who'd want a boy like that?" Vincent's grand-mother sniffed. "Which isn't to say he may not improve in time, although I'm not convinced as yet. I put him in charge of getting rid of the rats in time for the ball tomorrow, and all he did was call for the rat catcher and scream every time he saw a trap. No—you've put your finger on the spot, my dear. I still haven't made up my mind. Thought I'd have a look around this morning and see if anyone caught my eye, but I can't say that any one of them stands out from the rest. They're all pretty, and they're all polite . . . and all as dull as dishwater." Realizing that this comment was not entirely tactful, she hastily added, "Don't mean *your* girls, of course."

"I think you should go on looking." Queen Kesta

spoke firmly. An interesting possibility was establishing itself at the back of her mind. The mother of seven daughters always has to be aware of every opportunity. "You should look at the girls here very carefully, whether they come from Wadingburn or . . . or somewhere else. Perhaps you could even arrange for a little parade as they leave? Or a test or two. Perhaps I could help you? I'd be very happy to think of some ideas. A demonstration of needlework? Recitation of inspirational poetry? Then later today we could have a chat and see which princess impressed us most."

Queen Bluebell gave her friend a sideways look. "Hmm," she said. "I'll think about it. You're a good woman, Kesta, and I could do worse than one of your girls. I promise I'll bear it in mind. Not at all sure I want to leave Wadingburn in the hands of a queen who recites inspirational poetry, though. Could cause mutiny among the peasants. ATCHOOO! Oh, this *dreadful* cold! Addling my brain, just when I need to be able to think. Come and try some cake, and tell me which one to choose for tomorrow. . . ."

As the booming voice moved away, Evangeline decided she could risk stretching her very cramped limbs. Behind her she could hear Mrs. Cringe whispering urgently to someone, and the Grand High Witch

frowned. Any noise could be dangerous, and this was most irresponsible. As she turned to hush Mrs. Cringe, she became aware that she was being stared at . . . stared at by the owner of a sharp nose, long whiskers, and extraordinarily sharp teeth.

"Ho, ho, HO!" said the rat, and he winked seductively. "What's a pretty little thing like you doing in a place like this?"

Chapter Twelve

Gracie was whistling as she and Gubble trudged down the track that would shortly take them into the village of Gorebreath. Despite the fact that they had had very little sleep, she was feeling remarkably cheerful and had almost convinced herself that the shadow on the loom would turn out to be nothing too serious after all. "Still," she told Gubble, "we should tell Marcus about it, don't you think?"

"Ug," Gubble agreed without having much idea what Gracie was talking about. "Dog."

"What?" Gracie looked at him in surprise. "What dog?"

Gubble waved an arm. "Dog, dog, dog. More dog."

Gracie listened, but the troll had sharper ears than she did, and she could hear nothing. "Don't worry. I like dogs, and they like me. I expect it's chasing a cat somewhere in Gorebreath. We're nearly there now. It's probably best if we go straight to the marketplace." Gracie took Gubble's hand and swung it as they walked. "Oh, Gubble! Is it very bad of me to feel excited? I know there's Deep Magic somewhere, and that's serious, but it's been ages and ages since I've been here . . . and we'll be seeing Marcus soon. And maybe Marlon too—" Gracie stopped. She could hear the sound of barking now. It wasn't the sound of a dog wanting its breakfast or a dog seeing off an intruder. It was the sound of hunting dogs baying as they searched for a trail, and a shiver ran down her spine.

Gubble nodded as he saw her expression. "*Bad* dogs," he remarked. "Hide!" And he stomped off toward the bushes and trees beyond the grassy verge edging the track. Peering around a tree trunk, he said encouragingly, "Safe here!"

Gracie looked after him, then gave herself a little shake. *Come along, Gracie Gillypot,* she thought. *Even if they are bad dogs, they aren't looking for you. If you're frightened by a few dogs, whatever will you do if you come across Deep Magic?* She took a big breath and called, "You go that way, Gubble. I'm staying here." Then she straightened her back and marched on.

As she went she attempted a brave whistle, but as

the sound of the barking grew louder, the tune began to wobble, and by the time she had turned a corner and seen the dogs rushing toward her, she had no whistle left . . . until Snarler ran straight by her without giving her a second glance.

"Phew!" Gracie heaved a sigh of relief, and she skipped onto the grass to watch the rest of the dogs hurtling past. "There! Didn't I say they weren't looking for us?" And she gave the purple and perspiring Buckleup Brandersby a cheery smile and a wave as he thundered up the path.

Buckleup, wheezing hard, might not have noticed Gracie if she hadn't waved. He was purple with rage as well as exhaustion; there had been no sign of Loobly anywhere in Gorebreath, and after the dogs had upset three market stalls and helped themselves to a variety of sausages, ham bones, and cheeses, he had been forced to leave at some speed. In Buckleup Brandersby's head this had become Loobly's fault, and the fault of all orphans high and low wherever they might be, and he was muttering such hideous and terrible threats as he pounded away from Gorebreath that the leaves on the trees on either side of the path shriveled and fell off as he passed.

But then Gracie waved, and Buckleup saw a tall,

skinny girl in a bathrobe, her hair in straggly braids, with soaking-wet bedroom slippers on her feet. Every one of his very basic instincts screamed "Runaway Norphan." He discounted the fact that none of the orphans in his care had ever been known to enjoy the comfort of bathrobes or bedroom slippers; it was after ten in the morning, and in Buckleup's opinion anyone of Gracie's age still in her nightclothes had to be on the run. He lumbered to a stop and peered at her. The dogs, grateful that their master was no longer shouting and screaming at them, sat down at a safe distance.

"So who are you?" Buckleup inquired with what he fondly believed to be a disarming smile.

Gracie, taken aback that he had stopped to speak to her, hesitated, and Gubble grunted a warning from behind his bush. "Erm . . . I'm Gracie Gillypot," she said.

Buckleup, always on Orphan Alert, noticed the hesitation. "'Oo's your mother?"

Gracie saw the bushes behind Buckleup shaking and, knowing that Gubble was watching, thought it safer to reply rather than risk annoying this huge purple-faced man. "I haven't got a mother. Or a dad. I live very happily in the Less Enchanted Forest, though, and if you'll excuse me, I'm on a rather important—"

She had no time to explain further. Buckleup was trembling with excitement. He had lost one orphan, but now, without any help or assistance, he had found another . . . and a wondrous idea exploded in his head. With a shout of triumph, he grabbed Gracie. "GOTCHER!" he yelled, and, slinging her over his shoulder, he turned and set off at a run.

"Put me down!" Gracie screamed, and she kicked and wriggled with all the strength she had — but Buckleup's grip grew tighter.

"Shut it," he growled, and then, as Gracie showed no signs of obeying, he pulled his Orphan Snuffer from his pocket. Gubble, scrambling out of the bushes as fast as he could go, saw the Snuffer whirl through the air, followed by a most unpleasant thud — and Gracie's limp body was hoisted back over Buckleup Brandersby's shoulder and borne away at a steady jog.

Gubble stood frozen in the middle of the path. Two large tears rolled down his cheeks, and a massive sob shook his solid body. "Bad Gubble," he whispered. "Gubble not help. Gubble BAD." He took a few indecisive steps in the direction of Gorebreath and paused. "Gubble *think*," he said, and an expression of acute agony overspread his flat green face. Seeing a

puddle at the side of the track, he took off his head and dunked it in the muddy water. After a few moments he put himself back together again and smiled through the dribbles of mud. "Find Marcus!" he said. "Clever Gubble!" And he began to stump along the track at a determined trot.

Chapter Thirteen

Prince Marcus was having troubles of his own. He and Arry were safely back at Gorebreath, but his plan to leave almost immediately had been frustrated by his mother. Queen Mildred had been deeply shocked to see the twins returning early and insisted on reading them a long lecture on the Importance of Always Observing Royal Etiquette. Marcus wriggled and squirmed and tried to explain that they'd left for the best of reasons, but his mother took no notice and simply talked over him. After half an hour he was beginning to wonder if his only hope of stopping the tirade was to fall on the floor in a wild fit of remorse, but at last the queen ran out of breath. "So," she said, "I do hope that you will never do such a thing again. The two of you must write Queen Bluebell a letter of apology, and we'll send it by royal courier this afternoon."

Marcus's eyes lit up. "Or I could take it! With . . ." he tried desperately to think of another reason to convince his mother. "With . . . some roses!"

Queen Mildred looked at him in astonishment. "Marcus, dear, how extremely thoughtful of you! That would be most suitable. In fact, perhaps you both should go."

"I'd be much quicker if I went by myself," Marcus said hastily. "After all, we don't want to keep Queen Bluebell waiting."

His mother raised an eyebrow. She was not normally suspicious, but this concern for Queen Bluebell was distinctly out of character. "Marcus, dear — you're not planning anything, are you?"

Marcus dug his elbow into Arry's ribs, and Arry turned his grunt into a cough. "It's OK, Mother. Marcus is quite right. His pony's much faster than mine, and besides . . ." Arry blushed. "I was rather wanting to write Princess Nina-Rose a poem."

"How very, very lovely." Queen Mildred's suspicions melted away, and she beamed at her oldest son as she settled herself on a sofa. "Did you ask her if she'll dance with you at the Declaration Ball? You haven't told me anything about your visit this morning, you know. How was dear Bluebell? And who else was there? Was Nina-Rose as pretty as ever?" The queen nodded knowingly. "Perhaps dear Nina-Rose will be chosen as Bluebell's successor. Wouldn't that be just too lovely?"

Marcus, on the point of exploding, folded his arms and glared. "Shouldn't we be writing our letters?" he demanded. "Arry can tell you all about it after I've gone—can't you, Arry?"

Arry, who had sat down next to his mother all ready for a comfortable chat, saw the look in his brother's eye and leaped to his feet. "Er—yes. Yes, of course I can. That would be wonderful. I'll be back in a moment, Mother." And he followed Marcus out to their old schoolroom.

"Honestly, Arry," Marcus said as he dug out paper and pens, "you could have tried to stop her from going on and on and on like that. Do you want this stupid feather or not?"

"Nothing stops her once she gets started," Arry said with absolute truth. "You know that. If you hadn't wriggled so much, she'd probably have stopped sooner, but she thought you weren't listening."

"I wasn't," Marcus admitted. "Anyway—let's get these letters done, and then I'll go."

Arry gave him an anxious look. "Will you be back tonight?"

"Of course not!" Marcus stared at his twin. "I've got to ask Gracie to the ball before I go tearing off after your bird. Didn't Nina-Rose say something about it being seen in Flailing?" He reached up and took an old rolled-up map down from a shelf. "See? It's miles away."

Arry looked at the map doubtfully. "Are you sure you'll be OK? We're not supposed to go outside the borders."

"I've done it before," Marcus said. "Besides, it's not far from the House of the Ancient Crones. I'll ask Gracie to give me a hand. It'll be easier to catch the peacock with two of us."

Prince Arioso, heir to Gorebreath, shuddered. "If you say so. I can't think of anything worse than trailing around horrible forests full of scary animals and horrible trolls and—"

"Hey!" Marcus frowned. "Trolls are OK!" He tucked the map inside his jacket and sat down at a desk. "How do you spell *apologize*?"

Arry told him, and for a few minutes there was no sound except for the scratching of pens.

Then Marcus jumped up, waving his letter. "Finished!"

Arry glanced at his brother's handiwork and opened

his mouth to point out that there were at least five spelling mistakes and two large blots. Remembering how long it would take Marcus to correct these, however, he changed his mind and merely said, "Well done, bro—but maybe we should fold it up and seal it before Mother sees it."

"Whatever," Marcus said happily. Arry finished his own letter with several twirls and a flourish, and Marcus pounced on it. "I'll seal yours as well," he offered, and lit a taper. The smell of melting wax filled the air, and Marcus thunked down the royal seal with enthusiasm. "There!" he announced. "All done. I'll be off now. Don't forget to rumple up my bed tonight, Arry—and enjoy your two breakfasts!"

Arry nodded. "You will be back by tomorrow evening, won't you? Mother'll have fifty-nine spasms and a fainting fit if you aren't here in time to get ready for the party."

Marcus was already in the doorway. "No worries. I'll be back with handfuls of feathers by then. You get busy practicing your dance steps for Queen Bluebell's Declaration Ball!" And he was gone.

Arioso sighed. He found himself wishing that his tutor, Professor Scallio, was still living in the palace instead of in a cottage with his sister somewhere in the Less Enchanted Forest. The professor was the only person who had ever been able to direct Marcus's wilder ideas into more practical channels; King Frank and Queen Mildred made no impression on him whatsoever. If anything, they made him worse; Arry had noticed long ago that the more his parents put pressure on Marcus to conform, the more he refused to do so. Arry sighed again. He hated having to ruffle his hair and rush around, pretending to be his own brother, but perhaps it was a small price to pay for the bliss of dancing with Nina-Rose for an entire evening. He went to wash the ink from his fingers before going downstairs to give his mother a blow-by-blow account of the morning's visit, with certain careful omissions— notably the demand for a white peacock feather.

Chapter Fourteen

Marlon was frustrated. He had thought that he, Loobly, and Alf would arrive at Wadingburn Palace early in the morning, but he had completely failed to realize how slowly Loobly would travel once she thought they were out of danger. Years and years of being incarcerated in the orphanage washhouse meant that, for her, the outside world was a place of wonder, and she stopped to look at every plant and tree. She peered into rabbit burrows and whistled up at nests, and it was nearly lunchtime before they finally reached the back door of the kitchen.

Then, to Marlon's intense irritation, she refused to go inside. "No like meeting peoples," was all she would say when Alf asked her what was wrong.

"But you won't *be* meeting people, kiddo!" Marlon said in exasperated tones. "You'll be scrubbing floors and washing dishes and all that stuff. Lowest of the low. You'll be emptying all the rattraps, I expect, and—" Marlon stopped.

An expression of interest had flickered across Loobly's thin little face. "Rats?" she whispered.

"Horrid things," Alf chipped in. "But they'll be dead as doornails. Deader than . . ." His voice faded away as he saw the tears begin to roll down Loobly's cheeks. "Erm—that is—maybe some of them won't be as dead as all that."

Quick to seize the opportunity, Marlon nodded. "Loads of rats here, kid. Palace is heaving with 'em. Like rats, do you?"

Loobly smiled a watery smile. "Ratties is my friends. Was always kind to Loobly. Nicer than peoples." She pulled the pickled rat out from her pocket. "See? Poor Ratty. Was almost dead like doornut. But getting better."

Marlon very much doubted she was right but was too tenderhearted to say so. Instead he concentrated on his task of getting Loobly safely hidden away from Buckleup Brandersby and Truda Hangnail. "Just think," he said encouragingly, "you'll be able to rescue loads of his merry little mates if you work in the kitchens." Loobly's face brightened, and Marlon added hastily, "Make sure nobody sees you at it, kiddo."

Loobly's eyes widened. "Can tippytoe. Nobody sees Loobly on tippytoe."

As she tiptoed toward the palace by way of demonstration, the back door was flung open and a red-faced cook came storming out, waving a wooden spoon. In front of her scurried an undersize boy in an oversize apron who cannoned into Loobly with such force that he knocked her over. A string of sausages sailed up in the air and was caught by the cook with a triumphant grunt. Grabbing the small boy by his ear, she was about to haul him back into the kitchen when her eye fell on Loobly. "Oi! What do you think you're doing out here? There's a heap of pans waiting to be washed. Get back in that kitchen this minute!"

And before Loobly had any opportunity to protest, she was whisked inside with the now sniveling boy, and the door slammed shut behind her.

Marlon inspected a claw in a casual manner. "See how it's done, kid? One orphan, safe and sound."

Alf gazed at him in admiration. "How did you know the door was going to open at that exact moment, Uncle Marlon?"

"Intuition, kiddo," Marlon lied. "And now we'd better fly."

Alf, delighted to be included in the plan, puffed up

his very small chest. "Sure thing, Unc. Let's hit those crones!"

His uncle cuffed him, but not unkindly. "You said it, kid. Let's fly."

And they flew.

Chapter Fifteen

Evangeline Droop wasn't enthusiastic about rats when she was her usual height; in her present circumstances, being only a little taller than the rat in front of her, she was terrified. She screamed—then slapped her hand in front of her mouth, horrified at what she'd done. Fortunately, Queen Bluebell was in the middle of a spasm of nonstop sneezing, and the scream went unheard.

"Now, now," the rat said reproachfully, "that's no way to treat a guy." He grinned at Evangeline. "Busy this afternoon, are you?"

"Er . . ." Evangeline was quite unable to think of a suitable reply. A voice answered for her.

"What you got on offer?"

The rat blinked. There was something strange about this voice, something that made him feel edgy and uncomfortable. It was also a voice that expected an answer.

"Erm . . . us rats are having a big meeting," he said without enthusiasm. "Thought the young lady here might like to come with me." He nudged Evangeline in the ribs with a sharp elbow. "Just the two of us."

Evangeline swallowed hard. She knew that voice; it was Truda Hangnail's. It must have been Truda who had been whispering with Mrs. Cringe a moment or two earlier. Evangeline's heart began to beat much too fast, and without being aware of what she was doing, she edged a little nearer to the rat.

"What kind of meeting?" Truda insisted. "What's up?"

The rat had had enough. "What's it to you, lady? I'm talking to the pretty one. Taken a fancy to her, I have, and seems like she feels the same about me. So keep your nose out of our business, *if* you don't mind!"

There was a tiny puff of purple smoke, and the rat began to cough.

When he spoke again, his tone was very different. "'Scuse me. Sorry about that, lady. Didn't mean to be rude." He coughed again. "It's our leader, Brother Burwash, ma'am. He's gone missing, so it's voting time. Gotta pick a new leader, see?"

Truda gave him a sharp glance. "And who are you?"

"Brother Bodalisk, ma'am, at your service." The rat bowed to Evangeline. "*You* can call me Boddie, sweetheart."

The horrified Evangeline was saved from thinking of an answer. The sounds in the Royal State Room suggested that visiting time was ending, and a babel of voices drowned out any reply she might have wanted to make. Queen Bluebell, intermittently interrupted by ferocious sneezes, was wishing everyone a good journey home, and Prince Vincent was scurrying about, getting in everyone's way.

As the final footsteps departed, the queen heaved a loud, gusty sigh and remarked, "Thank goodness for that! ATCHOOO! Glad to see the back of them. Never seen such a lot of frilly-minded females in my life; couldn't say a word when I asked them what they thought about this year's hay crop or the price of peas. Not Kesta, of course. Good woman, even if she does talk too much. Vincent — stop shilly-shallying and go and do something useful. *ATCHOOO!* Find out if your rat catcher's doing his stuff. We've got rats everywhere, and it won't do. It won't do at all. Never bothers *me,* of course — I quite like the little fellows, in fact — but what'll our guests think if the place is running with rats tomorrow? They'll all be off home again, quick as a wink, and there won't be a single king or queen left to witness the Declaration." There was another loud sigh. "D'you know what, Vincent? I'm feeling my age. I never thought I'd say it, but I am. I'm surrounded by nincompoops frightened by nothing more than a set of whiskers and a scaly tail . . . *Atchooooooo* . . ." And her booming voice faded away as she sneezed herself into the distance.

At last there was no sound. The witches and the rat strained their ears, but there was an emptiness in the air. Brother Bodalisk took advantage of the silence to give Evangeline a quick squeeze, and she screamed again.

"What's that?" Prince Vincent, who had been brooding in the doorway, came clattering back. Bending down, he peered under the bookcase and was appalled to see six pairs of eyes staring back at him. Bodalisk had vanished.

"EEEEEEK!" Vincent's shriek echoed to the roof turrets of Wadingburn Palace, and the pigeons fluttered away. Servants came running from all directions, and the gibbering prince pointed with a trembling finger to the bookcase. "There!" he quavered. "Under there! THOUSANDS of rats . . . I saw them!"

"I'll get the catcher, Your Highness," said a tall footman as two of the maids jumped hastily onto chairs, and the others suddenly remembered they were urgently needed elsewhere. "I understand as he's having a cuppa tea in the kitchen." He marched off at speed. A second, braver footman bent down to see for himself, but a shaking Vincent pulled him away.

"They might run out!" he said. "Don't look! They're horrible! They might leap on you! They've got the beastliest whiskers and hideous teeth!"

The footman looked alarmed. "I'll tell the rat catcher to hurry up, Your Highness!"

As he strode away, Vincent climbed onto his grandmother's golden throne. One of the maids tittered, and he gave her a chilly look. "I can observe the rodents better from here," he announced.

Under the bookcase, Truda glared at Evangeline. "Now see what you've done!" she hissed, and reached into her pocket.

"Teach her a lesson, Grandma!" Mrs. Cringe encouraged, rubbing her hands together in glee. Evangeline, very pale, was beginning to stutter an apology when her hand was grabbed.

"This way, doll!" Bodalisk was back. "Quick! Follow me." And he led her swiftly toward a small opening at the back of the bookcase. With a squeeze and a wriggle, he disappeared. Evangeline hesitated. The hole was extraordinarily small and dark.

"Get on with it!" Truda said. "Here—let me go first!" She shoved Evangeline out of the way and followed the rat. There was the sound of a kiss and then a scuffle, but any comment from Truda was drowned by the noise the rat catcher made as he stomped into the State Room, accompanied by his yapping dog. Mrs. Cringe squeaked in terror and elbowed her way past Evangeline. She forced herself through the rat hole, and as the yapping grew closer, Ms. Scurrilous, Mrs. Vibble, and Mrs. Prag squeezed after her. It wasn't until the little Jack Russell terrier pushed his nose under the bookcase that Evangeline finally plucked up the courage to follow them . . . and found herself sliding into a blackness so profound that she couldn't see her hand in front of her face.

"That you, babe?" said Bodalisk's voice. "Welcome to *Chez Rattus Rattus*! But we'd better get going." There was a creaking sound as if a rusty door were being opened, and a dim light lit up the tunnel. "This way, gorgeous!" And Bodalisk frisked his way around the

other witches to take Evangeline's arm before walking her away along a twisty tunnel that led down and down.

Truda Hangnail snorted but said nothing. In the distance she could hear the sounds of many rats squeaking and murmuring, and there was a cold and calculating look in her sharp black eyes as she hurried along behind the Grand High Witch and her scaly-tailed companion. Her hand was in her pocket, fingering her bag of bones.

Chapter Sixteen

Gracie's head hurt.

She tried to open her eyes, but the stars circling her head twinkled so brightly that she shut them again. Someone dripped cold water on her face, and it dribbled down her neck; she sneezed, and a voice said, "Told you! I knew she wasn't dead. She's just been snuffed."

This time Gracie managed to open first one eye, then the other. She was lying on a bed so hard she had thought she was on the floor, and she was surrounded by a group of children with enormous hollow eyes. They were so skinny that the light from the dirty barred window almost shone right through them, but they were looking at her with interest.

"Where am I?" she whispered.

"Orphanage," said the tallest girl. "You should know that. You've lived here long enough."

"What?" Gracie turned her head to stare at the girl and winced. Her head was throbbing, and there were still a few stars dancing just beyond her vision. She was also extremely cold; her bathrobe had vanished, and her pajamas were muddy and damp. "What do you mean? What orphanage?"

"He said you wouldn't know where you were," said a small boy with sticking-out ears. He peered at Gracie. "Or who you are. And you *do* look ever so different. He said it was the witches did that to you."

Gracie's head began to spin, and not just with pain. "Witches? What witches?"

The tallest girl folded her arms. "Come on, Loobly Higgins." She spoke in a loud, clear voice as if she thought Gracie were deaf or simpleminded. "We know you aren't very clever, but even you must remember you've been up with the witches. Work experience, remember?" She leaned closer, and for a millisecond Gracie thought she saw a tiny wink. "You were let out for a week, and you ran away last night—"

"And Mr. Brandersby found you, but you didn't want to come back here, and so he snuffed you!" the small boy interrupted. He sounded as if he were thrilled by the excitement of it all.

"But you'll never run away again, will you, Loobly?"

The tall girl was now looking at Gracie very hard indeed, and again there was the suspicion of a wink.

"Erm . . ." Gracie's thoughts were whirling. Was she expected to agree? "No. No, I'm sure it's a very bad thing to run away."

"That's right!" The tall girl smiled, and it was obvious that Gracie had given the right response. "It's a *very* bad thing to run away."

"Very bad," Gracie echoed, and a bulky figure moved out of the dark shadows beneath the window. He was carrying a large, knobbly stick, and even Gracie cringed as he swung it to and fro.

"I'm glad you've seen sense, Loobly Higgins," Buckleup Brandersby growled. "Those witches didn't do you no good. No good at all. Turned your wits, what little you had of them. *And* changed your looks— and not for the better in my humble opinion. Still, I'm a fair man. You're back now, so we'll let bygones be bygones. You get down to that washhouse with Letty and set to work. And the rest of you"—he turned a burning eye on the other orphans and gestured with a clenched fist—"SCAT!"

The orphans scatted, with the exception of the tall girl. As she put out her hand to help Gracie to her feet, Buckleup Brandersby loomed over the two of them.

"Just you remember, Letty Higgins." He held the Snuffer warningly under Letty's nose as he pointed at Gracie. "This here is Loobly, and I hold YOU responsible for making sure as she remembers. That witchery's strong stuff. If she starts telling any tales as to how she's not Loobly, or she goes causing trouble, you'll be in for it. Get it?"

Letty shivered. "Come on, Loobly. It's socks today but—you remember that, don't you?" As she spoke she gave Gracie's arm a meaningful squeeze.

"Socks," Gracie repeated, and shivered in her turn.

"Good work!" Buckleup almost smiled. "Letty Higgins—I'll make something of you yet! Now—get away to that washhouse." And he opened the dormitory door with a mock bow and watched the two girls scurry away down the corridor. As they went, he pulled Gracie's package of cookies out of his pocket and crammed six into his mouth. "Very satisfactory," he told himself. "By the time those busybodies get to see her, she'll be answering to Loobly as if she were born to it." He gave a nasty chuckle. "Now, let's see if I can get a few pennies for that bathrobe. Nice bit of stuff, that robe." And he stomped off in the other direction.

* * *

Two elderly rats, who had been watching unseen from underneath a bed, shook their heads.

"That wasn't our lovely Loobly," said the bigger one. "Our Loobly's gone."

"That's a nimpostor!" the little one agreed. "Our Loobly does bring cheeses. Cheeses for us ratsies."

The bigger rat looked mournful. "What'll we do without her, Doily? That man—he'd eat the paper that wrapped the rind that covered the cheese before he'd give us anything."

"Us'll go hungry," said Doily, and two tears rolled down her nose. "Us'll be little starvy bones. Big bones for you, Sproutie, and little bones for me."

Sprout scratched an ear. "Maybe we could ask the impostor?" he suggested. "She wasn't our Loobly, but she didn't smell of wickedness. She smelled . . . she smelled good. And that's like our Loobly."

"Dunno." Doily thought about it. "Maybe. You do the askings, Sproutie. I be scared."

"We'll wait until she's safe in bed," Sprout decided. "The old man'll be away by then. If she does the Scream, she'll not be heard."

Doily looked at Sprout in admiration. "You be my hero, Sprout! But ain't you awaying? Meeting of ratsies?"

"Ah." Sprout scratched the other ear. "It's a long way, Doily. And we haven't eaten since our Loobly left. Reckon I'll wait and have a word with the impostor instead. Must look after my Doily."

Doily gave him a fond look and stroked his whiskers. "I do be wishing our Loobly were safe home, Sproutie."

Sprout sighed. "Maybe she'll come back. But then again, maybe she won't. We always knew there was something different about her, Doily. She's not like the others."

Chapter Seventeen

Marlon, looping steadily through the air, saw Alf suddenly zigzag, then zoom downward.

"Seen something, kid?" he asked. "Can't stop for sightseeing, y'know. Things to do, crones to meet—"

"Unc!" Alf's voice was even squeakier than usual. *"Look!"*

"What? Who?" Marlon flew in a swift circle but could see nothing unusual on the road below. They had reached the far side of Gorebreath; the market traders had been in a state of some agitation, but there had been no sign of anything sinister either there or elsewhere on their journey.

"There!" Alf pointed.

Marlon looked again and saw what appeared to be a green hillock at the side of the road. As he flew closer he saw it had legs and arms waving feebly in the air.

Faint cries of distress were coming from a nearby bush.

"Good work, kiddo." Marlon dived and saw that, as he had suspected, Gubble and his head had become separated. Marlon issued instructions, and after some confusion as to which was Gubble's left hand and which was his right, his two parts were reunited.

As soon as his head was properly in place, Gubble struggled to his feet and set off as fast as he could go, grunting as if he were in pain.

"You OK?" Marlon inquired, flying at his left shoulder.

"Urk," Gubble said. "Gracie. Thud. Marcus. URK!"

"Gracie?" Marlon, who prided himself on always staying cool and calm, looked flustered. He fluttered in front of Gubble's large moon face. "What thud? Who thudded? When?"

Gubble slowed, then stopped. "Gracie," he explained. "Man ask Gracie questions. Thud! Gracie carried away." He rubbed his eyes and sniffed loudly. "Gubble in bushes. Gubble BAD. Find Marcus!"

"Hang on." Marlon digested the information. "See any witches?"

Gubble looked blank.

"OK. No witches." Marlon beckoned to Alf, who

was hanging off a twig and twittering with excitement. "Kiddo—here's a problem. We've got witches, we've got Evil, we've got an orphan, and we've got a kidnapping. What's the deal?"

Alf, unable to help himself as a dazzling idea sprang into his head, did a sideways spin under Gubble's nose. "The man!" he squeaked. "Were there dogs?"

Gubble's small piggy eyes brightened. "Ug. Dogs!"

"That's it, Unc! We saw him!" Alf was spinning like a top. "On the hill! The orphanage man! With the scary witch!"

"Cool it!" Marlon glared at his nephew. "This is serious stuff, kid."

"But I'm right, aren't I?"

Marlon nodded. "Yup."

"So are we going to hunt him down and rescue Miss Gracie and tell Marcus—I mean, Prince Marcus—they can live happily ever after?" Alf began a final twirl but stopped halfway around when he saw his uncle's expression.

"Happly after." Gubble beamed at Alf. "Gubble like happly after!"

Marlon sighed deeply. "Hate to spoil the party, guys—but look at the situation. What have we got? One troll, two bats. That guy's big. What's more,

he's got dogs. And—correct me if I'm wrong—that orphanage place has bars. Steel bars. Best to get straight to the crones."

"But you've got brains!" Alf's eyes were shining with admiration and belief. "Uncle Marlon, you can do it!"

There was a short silence, then Marlon took a deep breath. "Kid," he said, "you're right. Duty calls. Never let it be said that Marlon Batster failed in his duty."

"Hurrah!" Alf cheered. "Hurrah! Hurrah—"

"OK, OK." Marlon stretched his wings. "You and the troll get to the orphanage. I'll wise up the prince and send him after you." He paused and eyed Alf and Gubble thoughtfully. "Don't mention the witch or Wadingburn Palace. Not at all. Don't want young Gracie involved in Deep Magic. Send her home, out of harm's way."

Gubble nodded. "Go home," he said. And then, "Boiled egg!"

"When are you coming back?" Alf asked anxiously.

Marlon held up one wing. "It's all in the plan, kid. No prob. Check the prince, report to the crones, back pronto. *Ciao!*"

Gubble watched the bat fly high into the sky, and nodded. "Happly after."

Chapter Eighteen

Gracie, having been brought up by a wicked stepfather and an evil stepsister, was used to hardship and hard work, but even she was taken aback when she saw the orphanage washhouse. Huge copper vats were seething and boiling, and the air was thick with steam that smelled hideously of sweat and dirt and dirty socks. Her head, still sore from the Snuffer, began to throb.

"It's dreadful!" she said as Letty hurried her in. "Do you work here every day?"

Letty shrugged. "Have to."

Gracie looked around as the older girl led her toward a huge stone sink. "Don't you ever want to escape?"

Letty shook her head. "Where'd I go?" She heaved a bucket up from the cold stone floor, tipped it into the sink, and began to scrub at the heap of sodden socks with a brush with very few bristles. "And don't you go thinking you can get out of here." She leaned toward Gracie and lowered her voice. "If you take my advice, you'll start thinking you're the one-and-only Loobly Higgins right now, this minute. Otherwise I'll be in for it—and I'm not going to take a beating if I don't have to!"

Gracie found another brush and set to work beside Letty. The older girl was looking fierce, and it was a few moments before Gracie plucked up the courage to ask the question that was burning a hole in her brain. "Excuse me—and I promise I'll try not to get you into trouble—but *why* does that man want me to be your sister?"

"Sister?" Letty stopped scrubbing for a moment. "What sister? I haven't got a sister."

"But he said Loobly Higgins, and you're Letty Higgins, so I thought . . ." Gracie's voice died away as an angry flush spread over Letty's face. "I'm sorry. Did I say the wrong thing?"

Letty glowered. "He calls us all Higgins. Says it doesn't matter, and it's easier to remember. I'm Liz Brownley, but he said that's a name for a person, and I'm nothing but an orphan, so Letty would do. Letty Higgins." Letty almost spat the name out. "No wonder nobody ever wanted to adopt me—not that he'd have let them. Loses him money if we get adopted. That's why you're here, of course."

Gracie frowned. "I still don't understand."

Letty heaved up an armful of moderately clean wet socks and dumped them in a second sink. "Loobly ran away. So he was scared he'd lose his shilling a week and his bread. But now he's got you, so you can be Loobly—and those stupid orphanage lady visitors will never know he lost an orphan." Letty grinned sourly. "Funnily enough, they get quite upset about that. Dunno why. They never get upset that we're all starving."

Gracie rubbed her nose with a damp finger. "So what's Loobly's real name?"

"No idea." Letty was wringing out socks as if she were trying to strangle them. "Not Higgins, that's for sure. She was dumped on the doorstep in a basket, and all she'd say was, 'Loobly dirty, Loobly dirty.'" She gave a sarcastic laugh. "That's why Fatso sent her to work in the washhouse. Ho, ho, ho, very funny—I don't think so. Poor little scrap couldn't even reach the sink! Now get on with those socks!"

Pushing a strand of wet hair out of her eyes, Gracie considered her situation. Things were not good, she decided. The orphanage was practically a prison; there were bars at every window, and the doors were heavy with solid iron locks. On the other hand, Gubble was somewhere not too far away, and presumably he'd seen her taken prisoner . . . or had he? Gracie swallowed as a vision of a miserable Gubble tied up in chains floated before her eyes. Could he have been captured too?

"Erm . . ." Gracie began. Letty was once again scrubbing socks, a grim expression on her face. "Erm . . . was anything—I mean, anyone—else brought in when I was?"

Letty raised her eyebrows. "Like what? Three mince pies and a kangaroo?"

"I was thinking more of a troll," Gracie explained.

Letty stared at her. "A *troll?* What kind of a girl are you?" She folded her arms and inspected Gracie from her feet to her head. "You know what? You really are a lot like Loobly. Odd. Do you talk to rats?"

"Not rats," Gracie said. "Well, not so far. I do have quite a few friends who are bats, though." She glanced up at a steamy window and sighed. "If they knew I was here, I'm sure they'd help me."

"Uh-uh." Letty glared. "I told you. None of that sort of talk. You try anything, and I'm in big trouble, and that means a LOT of trouble for you."

Gracie ignored the threat. "But you could come

with me, Letty! I'm an orphan, and the crones took me in. I'm sure they'd look after you too."

"I don't need looking after," Letty snapped—and then softened. "But thanks for the offer." Her shoulders drooped. "Sorry. You don't get much kindness in here. Only from Loobly. She was kind to everyone, even the rats." Letty bent down and fished about under the sink. "Look at this. The only thing she ever owned, and Fatso tried to take it away from her." She pulled out an old and battered shoe. It was extremely grubby, but the thought crossed Gracie's mind that it could have been made of silk, or even satin. "Poor little Loo," Letty went on. "She cried for days after he stole it—but I got it back. Snuck into his office and took it. Dunno what he wanted it for, except the shiny buckle. It was chucked in a bin by the time I found it. No buckle by then, of course."

Gracie smiled at Letty. "That was really kind of you. And he didn't see you?"

The older girl sniffed. "Never noticed. Loo and I found this hidey-hole under the sink so she could keep it safe."

"If it was so special, why didn't she take it with her when she ran away?" Gracie asked.

Letty's eyes opened wide, and she looked at the

shoe as if it might have some kind of answer before tucking it back in its hiding place. "I never thought of that. You're right. Hey! Maybe Loobly didn't run away! Maybe . . ." Her powers of imagination ran out. "Maybe she's *dead*!"

"But she might not be," Gracie said encouragingly. "Perhaps we could find out. If you wanted, that is."

Letty looked doubtful. "Don't see what we could do."

"Well . . ." Gracie hesitated. "Do you think there's any way I could get a message out of here? To a friend?"

"That'll be a boy, then."

"How did you know?" Gracie asked in surprise.

"You were blushing. Where does he live?" Letty tipped yet another bucketful of socks into the sink. "And keep working. If we haven't cleared these by the end of the day, there'll be no supper."

Gracie found herself blushing an even deeper red. "Erm . . . in the palace. Gorebreath Palace."

"One of the footmen, is he? Heard they're tall and tasty." Letty elbowed Gracie in the ribs. "Well . . . you might just be lucky. There's a pile of clean sheets going back there this afternoon. You could tuck in a note and hope it gets there."

Gracie's heart began to beat faster. Would a note

addressed to Prince Marcus ever reach him? She imagined the chambermaids giggling and throwing it away . . . or would they? It had to be worth trying. "OK," she said. "Where do I find a bit of paper and a pen?"

Letty looked furtively left and right, then dug in her pocket. She produced a torn paper bag and a stump of pencil. "Here you go. And it's that bundle by the door. See? The one with the label. You can tuck your note into the top."

Gracie took the pencil and paper, licked the end of the pencil, and wrote, "Dear Marcus, PLEASE HELP! I'm stuck in the orphanage." And then she stopped. Should she write, "Love, Gracie"? Or was that assuming too much?

"Hurry up!" Letty hissed. "The carrier'll be around any minute."

Gracie hastily wrote, "Yours, Gracie," and ran across to the bundle addressed to Gorebreath Palace. She was just in time; as she hurried back to her sink, a burly man came striding in. He swept up the bundle, along with three or four others, and heaved them onto his back. As he stood for a moment balancing his load, the note fluttered out and fell to the ground in front of him.

With a grunt he bent to pick it up, and a wide grin spread across his face as he read it. "Trying to get out, girls?" he said, and leered at Letty and Gracie. "So which one of you's Gracie?"

Gracie stepped forward at once. "I'm Loobly, and she's Letty," and she pointed to the older girl. "There's no Gracie here. Not that we know of."

"Hmph. We'll see what Mr. Brandersby has to say," the man said, and he waved the note in the air before tucking it carefully into a pocket. "Could be worth a pint of something for a poor thirsty man, this could. Bye-bye, girls!" And he marched out of the wash-house, still grinning to himself.

"Now look what you've done!" Letty was white with anger.

"I'm sorry," Gracie said. "I really, really am."

Letty gave her a cold stare, then shrugged. "At least you were quick enough with the names," she said grudgingly. "Here. We need to hang these up. I'll show you the way." And she led Gracie out into a stone-paved drying yard, where the surrounding walls were topped with broken glass. "Get pegging!"

Gracie, staggering under the weight of the basket of sodden socks, did as she was told. Her head was aching badly, and she was beginning to wonder if she was ever going to see her beloved crones again. She reached for a handful of pegs and began to peg sock after sock after sock onto the sagging clothesline.

"Hurry up," Letty said impatiently. "You'll have to be quicker than that! I'll go and get the next basket." As she hurried back into the washhouse, Gracie rubbed her eyes and reached for yet another sock.

High above the orphanage, a very small bat dived into a victory roll followed by two twirls and a triumphant spiral before zooming away.

Chapter Nineteen

Truda Hangnail was smiling, and it was not the sort of smile designed to make anyone feel happy. Evangeline could feel cold chills running up and down her spine, and Ms. Scurrilous and Mrs. Prag were trembling. Mrs. Vibble's teeth were chattering; even Mrs. Cringe shivered. Bodalisk was aware of an unpleasant tingling under his fur as he led the way out of the long tunnel and onto the top of a large water tank set high in the wall of the wine cellars of Wadingburn Palace. Below, in among the wooden casks and racks of dusty glass bottles, heaved a restless mass of rats.

"We can see better from here, ma'am," Bodalisk announced. "Not a lot of us are allowed on the tank, as it happens." He pulled on a whisker. "Just . . . just us seniors." He glanced at Evangeline to see if she was impressed, but she was staring down in horror. Bodalisk mistook her expression for admiration and smirked. "Fine body of brothers and sisters, ain't it? Could overrun the palace any day if we wanted, but we keep to ourselves."

"What was that?" Truda's eyes were gleaming. "How could you overrun the palace?"

Bodalisk looked at her in surprise. "We've got runs everywhere. Whole place is riddled with them. But there's no point in causing trouble. We go where we want, and we live as we please, but we stick to the Rule of Rat. Out of Sight and Around the Edge. Keeps the Large Ones happier that way."

"The Large Ones?" Evangeline asked faintly.

"*You* know." Bodalisk shrugged. "Humans. And Huwomans. People. There's a queen here, you know. This"—he waved an arm—"is a queen's house. The Large Ones call it a palace. Wadingburn Palace."

Evangeline gave the rat a feeble smile. "Fancy that."

Truda was stroking her whiskery chin and inspecting the milling hordes beneath her. Her expression was one of extreme cunning. "Who's the leader here?"

Bodalisk shook his head. "No leader, ma'am. Brother Burwash went missing, been gone for days now.

Shame . . . he was a good leader, he was. Now we've got to choose between Brother Squint, Brother Bolder, and Brother Mildew, and they're all three just as bad as one another —"

Ms. Scurrilous interrupted with an offended cough. "Ahem. Are there no — erm — sisters?"

"Sisters?" Bodalisk sounded appalled. "Certainly not!"

Truda cut in before Ms. Scurrilous could begin to argue. "So there's no other leader, then? No kings or queens, nor anything of that kind?"

"We rats are a democracy," Bodalisk told her. "We don't believe in inherited power."

"Hmm." Truda had her hands in her pockets. "Could be you're right, thinking that way. None of this la-di-da Bluebelly the Twenty-eighth nonsense for you, then."

Bodalisk was about to reply but was interrupted by a shrill whistle from the floor below. A well-rounded rat with self-important whiskers was climbing onto an old and battered cardboard box that served as a platform. "That's Brother Snirkles," Bodalisk whispered. "He'll open the debate."

Brother Snirkles blew again on his whistle, and the squeakings and mutterings faded into silence. "Brothers and sisters," he began, "we are here to mourn the passing of Brother Burwash."

"Wail! Wail for Brother Burwash!" called a shrill voice from the crowd.

"Hush, Sister Millifee!" Brother Snirkles looked angrily in the direction the voice had come from. "As I was saying before I was so rudely interrupted, Brother Burwash has left us. He has gone to the great rat heaven down below, where the sewers are filled with succulent bacon rinds and yellow-crusted cheeses and plump little raisins and—"

"Get on with it!" This voice came from another part of the cellar and was deeper in tone.

Brother Snirkles looked anxious and shifted from one foot to the other before continuing. "Yes, of course, Brother Squint. Whatever you say, Brother. Erm . . . where was I? Oh, yes . . . We are here to bid our leader farewell and to regret the manner of his passing—"

"Get ON with it, Snirkles!" The voice interrupted again. "We all know he's vanished. Missing, believed dead. Bad show and all that, but it's time to vote. Some of us have better things to do than to listen to you droning on and on and on. In fact, when I'm leader, we won't be having—"

"And who said you were going to be chosen,

Squint?" There was a sudden flurry at the side of the cardboard box, and an exceptionally bulky rat climbed up to join the unfortunate Snirkles. He folded his arms and gazed around. "What you need is me. I'm a plain-speaking rat, but I know what's what. Bolder by name, and bolder by nature. I'll take you rats where you've never been before, I will."

There was an interested murmuring, and Bolder grinned, showing a set of viciously sharp teeth.

"How many of you are aware that changes are in the air?" he demanded. "How many of you know that Queen Bluebell the Twenty-eighth, ruler of Wadingburn——"

"But not of us rats!" shouted a voice.

"Exactly. How many of you know that the ruler of Wadingburn is about to declare her successor?"

There was a muttering from the rats, and many heads nodded.

"We heard her talking last night," said one.

"And the night before," said another.

"Couldn't make up her mind at all," said a third.

"What's it matter, anyway?" asked a very small rat with very few whiskers.

Brother Bolder frowned. "It matters a great deal, my foolish friend. Bluebell may have left us alone, but a new time is coming upon us. We—who listen under floorboards and skulk behind skirtings—we hear these things. Already our runways and passages are fraught with danger, and traps are set that never were set before. Already the rat catcher is called for. Already the rat catcher's dog is sniffing and whining—"

"Wail! Wail for the ratcatcher's dog—"

"SILENCE, Sister Millifee!" Brother Bolder stamped his foot. "We will not wail! Our time for wailing is gone. Now is the time for action. Now is the time for us to rise against our oppressors, before it is too late!"

As Brother Bolder paused there were loud and enthusiastic shouts from the floor, as well as a good deal of air-punching.

"Vote for Brother Bolder!" yelled a voice, quickly followed by many others.

"Uh-oh," Bodalisk breathed in Evangeline's ear. "Brother Bolder's going to cause trouble. . . ."

"It's time to rise!" Brother Bolder began to march around the top of the cardboard box. "What have the Large Ones done for us? Are they not our enemies? Who among us has ever had kindness from a Large One? Who knows of—"

"Excuse me!" A single skinny arm waved in the air.

Brother Bolder stopped and stared in amazement. "What? Who's that?"

"Excuse me!" The owner of the arm was elderly and apologetic. "Sorry, Brother Bolder, very sorry—but it's Brother Brokenbiscuit here. I feel I ought to mention Loobly. . . . Loobly Higgins."

Evangeline Droop and Truda Hangnail jumped.

"She's been a real friend to me," Brother Brokenbiscuit went on. "And to my dear sister and her husband. A *best* friend, even though she is a Large One. Why, we've known her since she was a tiny girl, and she's never—"

"That's enough!" Brother Bolder was acutely aware that the militant atmosphere was fading fast. "One Large One is an exception, not the rule! Is she here? No! Is she cheering with us? No! Has she ever waved a flag on our behalf, demanding the end to all rat catchers and their fiendish dogs? I think not!"

"It would be difficult for her." Brother Brokenbiscuit was determined to be heard. "You see, she lives in the orphanage—"

"Then she's not here!" Brother Bolder snapped his fingers, and a couple of well-muscled young rats detatched themselves from the walls of the cellar.

With practiced ease they slid a paper bag over Brother Brokenbiscuit's head and whisked him away to a far corner of the cellar.

"And now, let's have a show of hands!" Brother Bolder looked around expectantly. "Who here believes our time has come? Who stands with me, to right our wrongs?"

"*I* do!" Truda Hangnail stepped forward. "I'll stand with you, if you'll stand with me!" And she pulled her hand out of her pocket.

The mist of purple floated into the cellar above the heads of the shocked and wide-eyed rats. Slowly it sank down, and slowly the rats' whiskers began to droop and their eyes to glaze over.

"Wail! Wail! Wail! Wa-a-a-a-a-a-a-a-a-a-a . . ." The wailing died away.

"Hey!" Bodalisk grabbed Evangeline's arm and hauled her into the tunnel behind the water tank. "What's she doing? What's that purple stuff?"

"Shh!" Evangeline whispered. "It's Deep Magic!"

"Deep Magic?" Bodalisk's eyes popped. "You don't want anything to do with that, doll."

"I know!" Evangeline stamped her foot in frustration. "But if I don't do what she wants, I'll never get back to normal. I can't stay like this!"

The rat blinked. "You look perfect to me, babe. But if there's anything I can do to help . . ."

Evangeline looked at Brother Bodalisk and saw that he was in earnest. It didn't seem likely that one romantic rat could save her and the entire kingdom of Wadingburn, but she thanked him before the sound of Truda's voice made her turn away from him to see what was going on.

"Rats of Wadingburn," Truda was chanting, "rats of Wadingburn, do you hear me?"

Every rat in the cellar turned as one to face the water tank. Brother Brokenbiscuit froze under his paper bag.

"We hear you."

"You will do as I say!"

"We will do as you say."

Truda cackled gleefully. "Now, my little ratty friends, listen to me, and listen carefully. I want to be Queen of Wadingburn—and what Truda wants, Truda gets. There's a party tomorrow, and by the time Bluebell stands to read her declaration, the people of Wadingburn will be begging me to take over, begging on bended knees, 'Be queen, Truda Hangnail, be queen!' Crying and weeping and wailing they'll be, every last king and queen and princess and prince, and why? Because if Bluebell doesn't declare me rightful queen, then the room, the palace, the kingdom, and the country—will be overrun with rats." She rubbed her bony hands together. "There'll be rats in the kitchens, rats in the halls, rats in the bathrooms, rats in the beds. Pick up a saucepan, and what'll they see?"

"Rats!" The response was unanimous.

"Turn back the bedcovers, and what'll they see?"

"Rats!"

"Step in the bathtub, and what'll they find?"

"Rats!"

There was another loud cackle from Truda. "When those pretty princesses go twirling and whirling—what'll they find hiding under their skirts?"

"RATS!"

"Good, my little scale-tails, good!" Truda's eyes were gleaming.

Evangeline, overcome with a mixture of terror and horror, could feel the old witch quivering with evil energy. There was a darkness hovering around her that was slowly freezing Evangeline's heart; when Bodalisk slipped his arm around her, she looked at him gratefully.

"And now, get busy!" Truda leaned forward, and the rats gazed up at her with their strangely blank eyes.

"Call your friends and relations, and bring them here. Bring them all, from the highways and byways. Bite and scratch, but make them come. We want every rat in the kingdom sneaking and skulking and hiding in corners, creeping and crawling and lurking in cracks, ready to leap out when I give the signal. And when I'm Queen of Wadingburn, it'll be parties for you all, each and every one of you—parties and fun every day." Truda raised her arms in salute. "You will be welcome everywhere. You have the word of Truda Hangnail!"

There was a riot of squeaking and squealing as the rats leaped up and down, cheering and yelling their agreement. Almost before Truda had finished speaking, Brother Bolder and Brother Squint were organizing rats into teams and issuing orders in total harmony with each other. Brother Snirkles hurried to assist them, and even Sister Millifee was seen exhorting her neighbors without so much as a wail.

Truda Hangnail nodded and turned to her companions. "Time to eat and to rest," she said. "We'll be busy tomorrow." And she chuckled unpleasantly before poking a sharp finger into Brother Bodalisk's back. "I need something to fill my old body."

"Yes, ma'am," Bodalisk said obediently. "There's

good pickings to be had in the dairy, ma'am, or you might prefer the kitchen?"

Truda considered the possibilities. "The dairy," she said. "Kitchens have cooks, and cooks are nasty. Of course, after tomorrow it'll all be mine, and *I'll* be telling the cooks what's what." She licked her lips in anticipation. "I'll be ordering cookies and cake and apple pie and cream until their hands drop off with cooking. And I'll be sitting on my golden throne ordering silks and satins and a diamond crown, and everyone will bow and scrape before they so much as speak to me." She cracked her knuckles and grinned so terribly that Bodalisk all but jumped off the water tank. "And if they don't do just as they're told, then I'll grow their noses down to their toes. I'll give them tails with scales and wither their bones. I'll make them dance to my tune — every minute of every hour of every day!"

If Brother Bodalisk wondered how this fitted in with Truda's promise that the rats would have the run of the palace, he said nothing. All he said was, "This way, ma'am," and he led the way down the tunnel and into a side passage.

Brother Brokenbiscuit quietly extricated himself from his bag and tiptoed unseen toward the entrance to the cellar.

Chapter Twenty

Prince Marcus of Gorebreath was humming as he rode through the marketplace. He had taken the precaution of borrowing a tattered old jacket and a well-worn woolen cap from Ger, the stable boy, and very few of his subjects gave him a second glance. They were much too busy arguing over the relative merits of carrots and cabbages and cauliflowers, or telling one another what they should have done (but hadn't) when Buckleup Brandersby's dogs ran wild amid the stalls that morning.

"Don't know what the place is coming to," said an old apple-woman indignantly. "Just like ravenous beasts, they were. Took one of my best hams, they did, and a string of sausages as well! And there'll be nothing paid for it. He's as mean as string beans, that man."

"Heard he was after a runaway," said her neighbor. "Caught her, too, by all accounts. Our Jem saw him marching along with the poor little thing slung over his shoulder with her braids a-swinging in the road dust. Dead to the world, he said she was."

"Not all he saw, either." A large red-faced butcher pushed in front of Marcus's pony in his excitement. "Told me there was a green-faced troll heading this way, large as life and crying its eyes out, and—"

"Excuse me!" Marcus interrupted. "Did you say a troll?"

The butcher put his hands on his hips and glared. "Mind your manners, lad! None of your business!" He turned back to the old women. "Jem took care of it. Said the troll asked him the way to the palace, if you please. So Jem asked it what business it had with the Royals, and when he didn't get any sense, he gave it a good hearty shake, and—would you believe it? Its head fell off! So he left it lying by the side of the road, and for all I know it's lying there still, and good riddance—"

"Excuse *me*!" Marcus pulled off his cap and did his best to look royal. "Where exactly is this troll?"

"I told you, laddie—" the butcher began, but one of the old women caught his arm, and whispered in his ear. Frowning, he looked Marcus's pony up and down. Noticing that the saddle and bridle were of the very best quality and that Marcus bore an uncanny resemblance to the picture on the Gorebreath two cent stamp, he began to cough and splutter. "Didn't mean any harm, Your Highness, only it was difficult to see it was you under that there hat—"

"The troll!" Marcus snapped. "This could be urgent! Where is he?"

"Back along the road between here and the forest," the butcher stammered. "That's what Jem said, Your Highness—" But Marcus was gone.

He took Glee through the marketplace at a swift trot, and the moment the road was clear of stalls and barrows, he persuaded the pony into a steady canter. "Why was Gubble asking for the palace?" he wondered. "Something must be wrong! He hasn't left the House of the Ancient Crones since he got there. Maybe he's bringing a message from Gracie? But surely she'd send a bat; that'd be miles quicker."

A terrible thought made Marcus pull on the reins so hard that his pony skidded to a sudden halt.

What had that woman been saying about a runaway before the butcher got in his way?

Marcus went hot, then freezing cold. "Gracie!" he said out loud. "Could it have been Gracie?"

"Sure was, kiddo," said a voice in his ear. "Knocked out and carried off."

"Marlon!" Marcus jumped as the bat circled in front of him. "Where did *you* come from?"

"Been looking for you. Get that pony turned around. If we've guessed right, Gracie's behind bars."

Marcus snatched up his reins. "Bars? What bars? Where is she?"

"Orphanage. Ugly big building between Dreghorn and Wadingburn." Marlon took in Marcus's hat and coat and the saddlebag slung behind him. "Were you off somewhere?"

"The Less Enchanted Forest," Marcus told him. "Arry needs a white peacock feather, or Nina-Rose won't dance with him, and I was going to see Gracie and ask if she wanted to help me find one. But why was she in Gorebreath?"

Marlon shrugged. "No idea, kid. But get her home."

Marcus straightened his back. "I'll get her out of the orphanage, even if I have to bring in the army. And then we can go to Flailing—that's where the pea-cock is."

"Good plan," Marlon said approvingly.

As Marcus turned Glee, he asked, "Have you seen

Gubble? There was a guy in the marketplace talking about a troll. . . ."

Marlon grinned. "He'll be waiting for you, kiddo. Him and Alf together. Keep your fingers crossed they don't try to bust in before you get there and get slapped in irons. Now, how fast can that pony go?"

"Fast," Marcus said with grim determination, and Glee whinnied in agreement.

"That's the boy. Me, I'm off to the crones. Catch you later!" And Marlon was away before Marcus could ask him any more questions.

It was ten minutes later that Glee cast a shoe. Marcus, boiling with frustration, had no choice but to walk the pony to the one-and-only blacksmith in Gorebreath.

The one-and-only blacksmith was a slow and solid man, and no entreaties, offers of bribes, or royal promises could make him move any faster than he was used to moving. "You'll have yer pony when he's ready," he announced. "There's coals to fetch, and the fire to make, and the bellows to blow, and the iron to heat——"

"I'll fetch the coals," Marcus said, but the smith shook his head.

"There's ways and ways of doing things," he said.

"And my ways is the ways I like." He paused to rest on his shovel. "And I expect your ways is the ways that you like too. There's many a passerby who tells me that."

Marcus agreed and hastily said he was going for a walk before the smith could expound any more of his rustic homespun philosophy. By the time he got back, at least the fire was blazing, but he was forced to sit by the smithy door until the sun sank and the evening drew in.

It was almost dark by the time the blacksmith finally finished, and Marcus was aware that the first stars were already twinkling. "There you be," the blacksmith said at last, and Marcus threw himself into the saddle.

It'll be really, really late by the time I get to the orphanage, he thought. *Will Alf still be waiting? What if Marlon's right, and he and Gubble have done something stupid?* And with hideous visions of Gubble hung in chains while Alf squeaked helplessly nearby, Marcus set off through the streets of Gorebreath at a reckless gallop.

Chapter Twenty-one

Gracie was also watching the stars, through the dusty windows of Buckleup Brandersby's office; Buckleup was striding to and fro, his face purple with anger. The note lay on the table, and Gracie was trying to look innocent. Much to her relief, Letty had been sent off to the dormitories with nothing more than a stinging slap.

"So who's this Marcus, then?" the orphanage keeper asked for the tenth time.

Gracie said nothing.

Buckleup tried a different approach. "Trying to get out of here, are you, Gracie Gillypot?"

"If you please," Gracie said politely, "you told me I was Loobly Higgins, and I wasn't to forget it."

"Don't you try and be clever with me, miss!" Buckleup stared at her with bloodshot eyes. He knew it was Gracie who had written the note, but there was something about her clear-eyed gaze that was making him feel uncomfortable. Loobly had had the same effect on him; he was able to bluster and threaten, but he hesitated to use brute force. "I'll teach you to be fresh, young lady. You'll stay in the washhouse tonight, and every night afterward, until you've learned not to answer back."

Gracie dipped a curtsy. "Yes, sir."

"Right!" Buckleup jangled the keys on his belt and strode toward the door, pushing Gracie in front of him. "Let's see how you like it down there in the cold and the dark when there's no one around to keep you company."

Gracie didn't answer. It wasn't until the huge wooden door had slammed behind her and the key had clicked in the lock that she finally took a deep breath. The washhouse was silent now, and a chilly dampness filled the air. Gracie shivered as she looked around.

"I'm not going to cry," she told herself. "Maybe this is all for the best; at least I'm on my own." She studied the windows, wondering if any of the rusty bars could be loosened, but they were much too deeply embedded in the solid stone walls. She pushed at the door to the drying yard, but that was locked as well as bolted.

So what do I do now? she asked herself. *I can't find a way out, so . . . so maybe I'd better get some sleep. Things'll look better in the morning—at least, I hope they will. They can't look any worse.* A thought struck her, and she smiled to herself. *Actually, they could be a whole lot worse—imagine if I was back living in Fracture with a horrible stepfather and being shut in a totally black cellar every night.* Gracie began to feel almost cheerful. *And Gubble will be looking for me.*

She yawned again and found her way to a pile of socks that were already washed and dried. Curling up among them, she did her best to think of glowing fires, and mugs of hot chocolate, and warm, cozy blankets, until she forgot about the cold stone floors and walls and drifted off to sleep.

Alf, tapping gently on the window an hour or so later, was unable to wake her. "Just like in the stories," he told himself with a romantic sigh. "Sleeping while she waits to be rescued." He flitted off to encourage Gubble, who had stopped some way down the road.

"Hurry up," Alf called, but Gubble held up a hand.

"Horse," he said. "Horse coming fast!"

Gubble was right. Seconds later Glee came galloping toward them.

"I'm sorry I'm late," Marcus said as he slid from his panting pony. "Is she OK?"

Alf waved a wing at Gubble. "Only just got here ourselves," he said. "That troll takes his time. And she's asleep." He looked hopefully at Marcus. "You could wake her with a kiss."

Marcus looked horrified. "I'd frighten her to death," he said. "Besides . . ." he pointed to the looming bulk of the orphanage, hideous even when painted silver by the moon. "We're supposed to be getting her out, not getting us in."

"She won't wake up," Alf told him. "I knocked on the window, but she didn't hear me."

"I could chuck something at it and break the glass," Marcus suggested, then shook his head. "Silly suggestion. Too noisy. Sorry. Guess I'm tired."

Gubble suddenly sat down. "Gubble sleep," he announced, and closed his eyes.

"Oh, no!" Marcus said, but Alf flew an excited circle.

"I know! You could both sleep," he squeaked. "I'm like Uncle Marlon. I'm good at night. You sleep, and I'll keep watch!"

Marcus yawned. "If you're sure . . . but wake us the minute Gracie wakes up."

Alf puffed himself up proudly. "Sure thing!" he said, and he flew to take up his position outside the wash-house window.

A minute later, he too was fast asleep.

Chapter Twenty-two

The witches of Wadingburn were huddled together in a corner of the Wadingburn Palace dairy. In front of them were three old cheese parings, one moldy crust and a bacon rind that had definitely seen better days. Bodalisk had presented the meal to Evangeline with a flourish, and she had done her best to be grateful, but it was difficult.

Truda Hangnail took one look at the meager offerings and snapped her fingers. She started to grow upward and outward, and Brother Bodalisk, sitting on the cold stone floor beside Evangeline, squeaked in horrified astonishment. Truda ignored him and began to help herself from the dishes of cream and freshly churned butter and plates of rich yellow cheese that were laid out in rows on the dairy shelves.

"This is the stuff for queens," she said with relish.

"If you don't mind my saying so," Ms. Scurrilous objected, "that hardly seems fair. Could you pass us a little cheese?"

"I do mind," Truda snarled, and pointed a bony finger.

Ms. Scurrilous said no more. Her ears were itching unbearably.

"This time tomorrow, the princesses will be arriving," Truda gloated as she continued eating, "along with the queens and kings and all . . . and won't they be in for a surprise!" She helped herself to more cream. "And once I'm given that crown, the Deep Magic'll flow . . . flow and flow . . . and grow and grow." She snapped her fingers a second time, and a flurry of purple sparks shot up into the air. A second later they were tiny purple wasps buzzing around and around the dairy.

Malice, who had been sulking ever since he was shrunk, opened one wicked eye to watch as Mrs. Prag and Mrs. Vibble scurried under a stool.

"See?" Truda cackled in triumph. "Be very, very careful, my little witchy friends. And now I'm off to sleep, and a future queen doesn't sleep on the cold stone floors of a dairy." She cracked her knuckles and peered out the dairy window. "There's a hayloft above the stables. That'll do for now. Where's my granddaughter?"

"Here, Grandma!" Mrs. Cringe stepped forward eagerly.

"You come with me. I'll need messages run in the morning. As for the rest of you — don't you go getting any fancy ideas!" And, pulling her black hood over her head, Truda slid out into the darkness, her tiny granddaughter scuttling behind her.

"What about us?" Ms. Scurrilous called from the doorway, but there was no answer.

"Got a cozy little nest under the churn," Brother Bodalisk offered.

The witches trailed after him, only to find that a cozy little nest for one was a bit *too* cozy when shared between four. There was a good deal of muttering and shoving before they settled down.

"Shall I sing you a lullaby?" Bodalisk asked.

"No," snapped Mrs. Prag.

"No, thank you," said Evangeline, more kindly.

"Okeydokey." The rat waved and slipped away to see what was going on in the palace. It was late enough for most of the Large Ones to be in their rooms, and the cavernous kitchen was almost empty. Just one small kitchen maid was left struggling with the last of a heap of frying pans.

Bodalisk eyed the obvious preparations for the next day's party with interest; there would be good pickings afterward. There was an enormous birthday cake covered all over with blue and silver icing on one table and a host of other smaller cakes on another. He was considering the chances of making off with a mouthful of fruitcake when a small voice said, "Ratty? Be you hungry?"

Brother Bodalisk froze. How could she have seen him under the dresser?

"Here you be, ratty, currants . . . currants for my dearly ratty. Be you better now?"

There was a faint answering squeak but no sign of any currants appearing on the floor, and Bodalisk relaxed. There must be another rat. He peered out cautiously and saw that the skinny girl was gazing earnestly into the pocket of her oversize apron.

"Weird," he decided. "Still . . . if she likes rats . . ." He took a step forward.

"Hello, more ratty," Loobly said. "Don't be frighted."

Bodalisk hesitated. There was nothing threatening about this girl; indeed, he felt as if he had walked into a patch of warm sunlight. He shook himself, and the lingering echo of Truda's purple Evil drifted from his mind, leaving him feeling wonderfully clearheaded. "Hi," he said, and bowed. "Brother Bodalisk. Pleased to meet you."

"Loobly," said Loobly. "And is pleased to be meeting too." She lifted a cover from a silver platter and took out a slice of fresh pink ham. "Here you be. Nicely for ratties."

"Wow!" Bodalisk said, and tucked it under his arm. "Thanks! Thanks very much!"

"No eating?" Loobly asked in surprise.

Bodalisk shook his head. "Got a lady friend," he explained. "I . . . I'd like to share it with her." He looked up at Loobly coyly. "Name of Evangeline Droop. Pretty name, ain't it?"

"Levangeline?" Loobly was wide-eyed. "But . . . is Auntie!" She shivered and crouched down by Bodalisk. "Listen, ratty. Listen to Loobly. Auntie Levangeline was magicked into littleness by badness. *Bad* badness . . . Loobly saw. Watch for badness, ratty. Is purple. Purple badness make things big and little and bad." She shivered again and glanced nervously over her shoulder. "Where Auntie Levangeline now? Is with scary witchy woman?"

Bodalisk, for the first time ever, was speechless. His eyes bulged as he stared at Loobly and took in what she was saying. It all made terrible sense: the purple mist that had cast a spell over the rats in the cellar, the way Truda had suddenly grown. . . . He swallowed. How had he not realized what was happening? He had known it was Deep Magic—hadn't he told Evangeline and tried to protect her? But somehow it hadn't seemed to matter very much—somehow he had gone along with Truda. Slowly Bodalisk realized that he too had been under Truda's spell, and a sense of righteous indignation made his whiskers tremble. He sat up straight and folded his arms. "As it happens," he said, "Evangeline's in the dairy, and the witch is in the hayloft—but don't you go out there. Could cause no end of trouble."

Loobly went very pale. "Must run away," she said. "You run, ratty. Is terrible badness coming. . . ."

"Hang on." Bodalisk regretfully put down the piece of ham. "I'm off. Going to find out what's going on, I am. Can't have my babe messed around with by that old trout. She's got a plan for tomorrow night; going to be queen, she reckons. You stay here." And Bodalisk, still bristling with indignation, slid under the kitchen door and disappeared in the direction of the hayloft.

Loobly looked up at the night sky. "Where be Mr. Marlon?" she asked. "Where be Alf? Where be crones? Oh, Loobly . . . bad Loobly. Should have gone to crones like Auntie Levangeline was asking." She sighed, and a tear trickled down her face and dripped off her chin. "And where be my dearly Doily? Where be lovely Sprout?"

Chapter Twenty-three

It was well past midnight in the House of the Ancient Crones, and the Ancient One was studying the web of power over Elsie's shoulder. The purple stain was intensifying and was in danger of spreading across the full width of the material.

"And if that happens," the Ancient One said, "all of the Five Kingdoms will be threatened." She sighed and readjusted the cat on her head. "I'll see how it looks in the morning."

There was a tap at the window, and she looked up to see Marlon grinning at her.

"Marlon!" she said as she opened the window and let him in. "At last! Have you seen Gracie?"

"No worries," Marlon said, settling himself comfortably upside down on the curtain rod. "She's being rescued by the prince and the troll."

"Rescued?" Elsie stopped weaving for a moment. "Oh, Marlon! Did the Deep Magic get her?"

Marlon shook his head. "She was popped into an orphanage, but I've sorted it out. Left Alf in charge." He paused to smile proudly. "The lad done good. This time tomorrow, Gracie'll be back here, safe and sound."

Room seventeen gave a convulsive shudder, and Marlon looked alarmed. "What's that?"

"The House is upset," the Ancient One told him. "Marlon, have you seen any sign of Deep Magic?"

The bat nodded. "I got Gracie well away," he boasted. "Some dame was up on Wadingburn Hill last night; purple mist 'n' all sorts. Threatening to take over as Queen of Wadingburn. Nasty piece of work. I came here to file a report; she's got the witchy women running all over the place. Not that they'll be any trouble. They're rat-size. Flash of blue light, and a few minutes later, down they went. But she's serious stuff."

He stopped. Both Edna and Elsie were staring at him. "Blue light?" they said together.

"Sure thing." Marlon was emphatic. "Blue all over."

"And Gracie was nowhere near," the Ancient One said thoughtfully.

Marlon shifted on the rod. "There was a kid hiding. Runaway orphan. The dame was after her, and the fat guy from the orphanage. Funny kid." The bat modestly studied a claw. "Rescued her, too. Damsel in distress, see?"

Elsie clapped her hands. "You're a hero!"

"Marlon," the Ancient One asked, her one blue eye shining, "could this girl be a Trueheart?"

"What?" Marlon considered for a moment. "Yup. Guess so." He went on thinking. "There was trouble with the dogs; ran into a purple kinda spell. The kid was up above in the tree, and as soon as the witch tried something—bang! Blue light everywhere, and they were up and at 'em again."

Elsie nodded. "Definitely a Trueheart. No doubt about it."

"Marlon," Edna said slowly, "I think there could be a way to defeat this witch . . . but I'll need your help."

The bat puffed out his furry chest. "No prob."

"I must ask you to be a hero for a second time." Edna gave the web a quick glance. "I want you to bring this girl and Gracie together. Two Truehearts together make a powerful combination and can alter the path of Deep Magic so it does little or no harm."

"Cool," Marlon said cheerfully. Room seventeen gave an immediate ripple, and he slid from one end of the rod to the other, flapping his wings indignantly. "Hey! What's with the shaking?"

"It's a Trueheart House. It's trying to send you on your way," Elsie told him. "It's a good sign, really. It means it thinks you can help."

The bat was still ruffled. "If you say so. And yup. I can get the kids together. But . . ." he paused. "That dame's dangerous . . ."

"And you're worried about Gracie," the Ancient One completed his thought. "I can't promise she'll be safe. Where Deep Magic's concerned, nothing and nowhere is safe. Not even here. But I know Gracie would want to do all she could to help."

"Check. Me too." Marlon stood at attention, but the effect was lost as he tried to hide a yawn and wobbled.

"You're tired." Elsie nodded at him sympathetically. "We won't expect you to fly all the way back, will we, Edna?"

There was no time for an answer. Room seventeen gave another violent shake, and Marlon found himself tossed through the open window. A gust of wind caught him and sent him high in the air, only to drop him on the path that was snaking around and around the outside of the House.

"Oi!" Marlon said, but already the path was off, carrying him with it at a breathless speed. Up the hill it raced, past bushes and bogs and in and out of trees, until the bat was so dizzy he was forced to shut his eyes. On and on they went, scooting through the Less Enchanted Forest and zooming through the Pretty Normal Forest until the path finally slithered down along the road that led to Wadingburn village. With a twist and a roll, it dropped its passenger in a heap with the sticks and pebbles and leaves it had gathered on its way, rippled a farewell, and vanished as speedily as it had come.

Marlon staggered to his feet amid the rubbish. A white feather, half buried, caught his eye, and he picked it up and inspected it. "Whoa," he said in surprise, and he tucked it under his wing before dusting himself off. Surprised to find that his tiredness had vanished, he chuckled. "What a way to travel! Excellento. Best be off. Check the orphanage, then on to the palace!" And he was gone.

Chapter Twenty-four

Gracie awoke with a start and for a moment couldn't remember where she was. There was a faint light attempting to brighten the windows, and she decided it must be early in the morning. She stretched and flapped her arms in an effort to warm herself up, but she felt chilled to the bone. A tear trickled down her nose, and she wiped it away crossly with her pajama sleeve.

"It would be easier to be brave if I had something to eat," she said out loud. "I'm starving. It feels like days since Gubble and I had those berries."

A thought struck her, and she went to look in the hiding place under the sink that Letty had shown her. Perhaps Loobly had a secret store of cookies? But there was only the old shoe and a broken wicker basket. Gracie pulled out the shoe, and looked at it again.

"That's our Loobly's," said a shrill voice. "Don't you go taking what isn't yours!"

Gracie jumped and looked around. At first she could see nothing in the shadowy light, but a moment later an elderly rat appeared on the draining board beside her.

"I'm so sorry," Gracie said. "I wasn't going to take it away. I was looking for something to eat."

The rat sat up and inspected her. "You're not a Screamer, I see. Hmph. That's a surprise." He pulled at a whisker. "Our Loobly wasn't neither, but then she was used to us. Knew her from a baby, we did. Erm — didn't find nothing to eat, then?"

Gracie shook her head. "No. Are you hungry too?"

"Hungry?" The rat rubbed his stomach, and it gurgled gently. "Hear that? Thinks my throat's been cut." He came a little closer. "It's the wife, though. She's the one I'm worried about. She doesn't get around as fast as she used to, so we don't go skittering through the kitchens anymore. Loobly used to bring us bits and pieces after her dinner, see, and we got used to it. Lazy, I suppose."

"She sounds very kind," Gracie said. "Do you know what happened to her?"

"She was awayed by the witchy women, our Loobly

was." The second voice was so high-pitched that Gracie had to strain to hear the words. A small, stout lady rat came shyly out from a hole behind the sink. "She be gone, and we be sadly without, ain't we, Sproutie?"

"There there, Doily." Sprout put his arm around his wife, and Gracie smiled at the two of them.

Doily came a little closer to Gracie. "You do smile like my Loobly. She did smile like summery days when she be happy, and she be happy with me and Sproutie."

"Was my Doily taught Loobly to talk," Sprout said proudly. "Couldn't say nothing at all when she arrived, so little she was. Just her name and how she was dirty."

"Letty told me about that." Gracie rubbed her nose. "And that she was in a basket with her shoe."

Sprout nodded. "Pretty little thing. All dressed up, too. Frills everywhere, weren't there, Doily?"

Doily sighed. "Lovely frilleries." She gave Gracie a hopeful look. "You be finding our Loobly?"

"I've got to get out of here first," Gracie said. "And I'm not—"

Tap!

Something tapped at the window, and the rats and Gracie swung around. A small black shape flapped cheerfully outside the dirty glass—and Gracie gasped, laughed, and ran toward it.

"Batsie!" Doily sounded nervous.

"It's my friend!" Gracie was already climbing up to see if she could unlatch the window, but the catch was welded up with rust and age. "Oh, well," she said, and picked up a scrubbing brush.

The glass broke with a sharp tinkling sound, and Alf flew in, tumbling into loop after loop in his excitement. "Oh, Miss Gracie!" he squeaked. "Are you OK?"

Gracie beamed at him. "It's *so* lovely to see you. Oh—might I introduce some new friends? Mr. . . . er . . . Sprout and Mrs. Doily?"

The two rats and the bat eyed one another for a moment before Sprout nodded. "Hello," he said with a certain caution.

Alf flew a series of tight spirals over Gracie's head. "Guess who's outside waiting for you?"

"Gubble!" Gracie clapped her hands.

"AND Prince Marcus!" Alf spiraled once too often, misjudged his landing, and ended his flight in a sink full of half-washed socks. "Oooof!" Gracie rushed to help him, but before she reached the sink, Alf emerged, sneezing. "So now we can have a happy ending, 'cause the prince has come to rescue you!"

Doily scampered forward and held up her paws imploringly. "Girlie—nicely girlie—prince be rescuing our Loobly too?"

Alf shook himself. "Loobly Higgins?"

"You know she?" Doily looked at the little bat in surprise.

"We rescued her." Alf tried to look modest. "Me and Uncle Marlon. We saved her from . . ." He suddenly remembered he wasn't supposed to mention Truda Hangnail. "We saved her from the orphanage man, and now she's safe in Wadingburn Palace kitchen!"

"Wow!" Gracie gave Alf a thumbs-up. "That's amazing! You're a star, Alf!"

Alf blinked and blushed under his fur. Sprout and Doily fell into each other's arms. "She's safe," Sprout rejoiced. "Will she be coming home soon?"

There was a rattle of small stones against the window, and Alf zoomed into a spin, grateful for the interruption. "That'll be the prince! We've got to get you out of here, Miss Gracie."

Gracie heaved a sigh of relief. "Thanks. D'you know what? If only I could get out into the drying yard, you might be able to help me find a way to get over the wall."

"I know!" Alf shot toward her, his little eyes

sparkling. "I heard it in a story! Sheets! You tie them together and make a rope and—"

Gracie shook her head. "But there aren't any sheets. There's only socks."

There was a pause. Even the indefatigable Alf could see that knotting heaps of damp woolen socks together might be impractical, but then Gracie jumped to her feet, her eyes shining. "I'm so stupid!" she exclaimed. "The clothesline! It's strong enough to hold loads and loads and *loads* of washing—I'm sure it'll hold me!"

"So all we've got to do is open that door!" Alf waved a cheerful wing at the heavy wooden door, firmly locked with a massive iron lock—and then looked again. "Oh," he said sadly. "Oh, dear."

Sprout coughed. "Ahem. The key's on that top shelf. Saw him hide it there myself."

It took Alf only a moment to push the key off the top of the dresser.

Gracie caught it and hurried to the door. "Freedom!" she said, but the large iron key was stiff and resisted all her efforts. Alf's encouraging squeaks did not make it any easier; Gracie grew hotter and crosser by the minute as she tried to turn it in the lock. "It . . . just . . . won't . . . work!" she puffed, leaning against the wall while she rubbed her aching wrist.

There was a scrabbling noise, and a whiskery nose appeared beneath the door. The nose was followed by a head and finally a body. The rat shook itself, stroked its whiskers into place, and gave Gracie a shortsighted smile. "Loobly, my dear," he said, "whatever are you doing? Have you forgotten? The key turns the other way."

"What?" Gracie came out from the shadows, and Brother Brokenbiscuit let out an agitated squeak. She tried the key once more, and the door opened. Alf cheered loudly, while Sprout and Doily came hurrying to reassure the elderly rat, who was clutching at his heart.

"She be goodly girlie," Doily told him. "Not our Loobly, but good."

Brother Brokenbiscuit began to breathe more easily. "Oh, Doily — a terrible, terrible thing is happening at the palace!"

Gracie, on the point of hurrying into the moonlit drying yard, stopped to listen. Alf, remembering his uncle's warning, looped a loop right under her nose. "No time, no time," he twittered. "Got to get you out of here and back home!"

"But what's going on at the palace?" Gracie asked.

Brokenbiscuit began to quiver. "Queen Bluebell's in trouble—"

"La-di-da, la-di-da!" sang the desperate Alf.

Doily peered anxiously at Brokenbiscuit. "Trouble for Loobly? Loobly be goodly queen."

Gracie, puzzled, bent down to hear Doily better. "Loobly? A queen?"

Doily shook her head. "Not our Loobly be queen." She frowned as she tried to make herself clear. "Be *other* Loobly."

"She means Queen Bluebell the Twenty-eighth is a good queen," Sprout interpreted.

"Oh. I see." Gracie pulled at the end of her braid as she remembered the ominous purple stain on the web of power. "And she's in trouble? What kind of trouble?"

"We've got to GO!" Alf twirled in the air like a tee-totum. "Marcus is waiting! He's been there *ages*! You can't keep a prince waiting! He's waiting for *you*—"

To Alf's profound relief, Gracie jumped to her feet. "I'd better go. Good-bye, Mrs. Doily. . . . Good-bye, Mr. Sprout. Please don't worry—if there's anything wrong at the palace, Marcus is sure to know about it."

As Gracie hurried out into the drying yard the

three rats stood on the doorstep, Brother Brokenbiscuit talking earnestly and waving his arms. He was still talking as Gracie undid the clothesline and Alf carried one end of it over the wall to the waiting Marcus and Gubble.

It was only as Gracie was climbing out of sight that Brokenbiscuit finished his story and Doily was finally able to speak. "Sproutie! Our Loobly be at queenly palace now," she said. "And I be so sadly without. . . . Shall us go too?"

Sprout pulled at his whiskers. "It's a long way."

A tear rolled down Doily's face. "But we is lonely." She gave Sprout a sideways look. "Loobly did leave her shoe. Will be missing he, like we be missing she."

Sprout straightened his shoulders. "We'll take Loobly her shoe," he said. "Brother Brokenbiscuit, will you help us? Loobly'll make sure no harm comes to us."

Brokenbiscuit began to tremble, but he nodded.

"Us be adventuring," Doily announced happily, and the three rats scampered back into the washhouse.

Chapter Twenty-five

The shards of glass on the top of the wall did not improve the state of Gracie's pajamas. Halfway down the washing line, she suddenly wondered if she was dressed the right way to meet a prince—particularly a prince she quite liked. Or, if she was honest, liked quite a lot. She was saved from any further thought by the line's snapping, and she fell the last couple of yards. She landed on top of Gubble, who grunted happily as he helped her to her feet.

Marcus smiled. "Hear you were kidnapped," he said cheerfully. "Nothing like that ever happens to me. You do have the very best adventures, Gracie Gillypot."

Gracie smiled back. "If you say so. Erm . . . thanks for rescuing me."

"And now, back to the Less Enchanted Forest!" Alf squeaked. "Time to go home!"

"Just a minute, Alf." Gracie turned to Marcus. "The rats—" She saw Marcus's startled look and went on, "Erm . . . Someone in the orphanage just told me Queen Bluebell's in trouble and that something terrible's happening at the palace. Have you heard anything?"

"'Scuse me!" Alf was flittering in circles, trying to catch Gracie and Marcus's attention. "'Scuse me—we ought to get going."

Marcus was thinking about what Gracie was saying. "Haven't heard a thing. All fine as far as I know. One Declaration Ball to take place tonight, complete with long, boring speeches; long, boring announcements; and twirly-whirly dances. Oh, did I tell you you're invited? If you want to come, that is."

"Really?" Gracie's eyes sparkled. "I've never been to a ball. It might be fun . . . and if there *is* any trouble, we could warn everyone."

"That's true." Marcus grinned.

"You ought to go home, Miss Gracie, you really ought." Alf was twittering faster and faster. An inspiration struck him. "I mean, you can't go to the ball in pajamas, can you?"

This was so undeniably true that Gracie stopped smiling. "You're right," she said. "I ought to go home—"

But Marcus intervened. "No! Let's go to Wadingburn!

We can't miss out on an adventure. We'll have to go to Gorebreath first—I've got to get changed—but that'll be fine, because you can borrow a dress or something, and we'll go to the ball together! I can't wait. . . . Let's get going!"

Alf gave a despairing squeak. "You can't! Uncle Marlon said! You've got to go home! He said—"

"Change of plan, kiddo."

"Uncle Marlon!" Alf gasped and collapsed in a small untidy heap on the edge of the road.

Gracie rushed to pick him up, and he lay in the palm of her hand with his eyes shut. "Is he all right?" Gracie asked anxiously. "Should I get him some water?"

Marlon flew around Marcus and Gracie and settled on Glee's saddle. "Kid'll be fine. Overacting."

Alf opened a reproachful eye. "I'm worn out! I tried and tried to make them go home! But you just said—"

"Change of plan." Marlon sounded unusually excited, and both Gracie and Marcus looked at him in surprise. "We're off to the palace instead."

Gracie noticed Marlon's expression. "Have you heard something? Is it about Queen Bluebell?"

"Unk." Gubble raised a fist.

Marlon nodded. "Big trouble." He paused for

dramatic effect. "There's a witch, and she's got her peepers fixed on Wadingburn Palace."

"A witch?" Marcus looked disappointed. "Is that all? You don't need to worry about the Wadingburn witches. They're a joke. They—"

"Nah. Different type. She's into Deep Magic. We've gotta flush her out before she takes over. She's aiming to be queen."

Gracie felt a cold shiver run up and down her spine. "Deep Magic. I was supposed to be looking for it. . . . It was on the web."

Marlon shifted from one foot to another. "Gotta talk business, kiddo. The crones say it's up to you. You and the other Trueheart—the Ancient says you can pull it off if you get together. When the witch makes her takeover bid, you 'n' Loobly can score. The witch'll go down."

"Just a minute." Gracie was trying hard to understand what Marlon was saying. "Are you saying you've seen the crones? Did you see Auntie Edna? What did she say?"

"Just told ya," Marlon said impatiently. "Two Truehearts—side by side. Powerful stuff!"

Butterflies began to dance in Gracie's stomach. "You mean . . . you mean Auntie Edna thinks Loobly and I can fight this Deep Magic?"

"You can do it, kiddo."

"I do hope I can," Gracie said, and she had to try hard to stop her voice from shaking.

Marcus grinned at her. "Hey," he said, "it's an adventure! Come on, Gracie Gillypot! We'll go to Gorebreath and get ready, and then we'll go to Queen Bluebell the Twenty-eighth's Declaration Ball. You can meet up with Loobly, and the witch'll explode or whatever, and it'll all end happily ever after." He banged Gracie on the back enthusiastically. "Good plan or what? And maybe you'll be declared the new queen!"

"Urk." Gubble suddenly grunted. "Gubble plan too. Gubble stay here."

"What?" Gracie and Marcus looked at him in surprise. "Why?"

Gubble folded his arms, and a grim expression spread across his flat green face. "Wait for man." He pointed toward the orphanage. "If man chase Gracie, Gubble BITE!"

"Hurrah!" Alf cheered loudly. "You show him, Mr. Gubble!"

"I don't think——" Gracie began, but Marlon interrupted.

"Excellento!"

Marcus nodded. "You know what? That could

work—if Gubble's sure that's what he wants to do. It'll be miles quicker if it's just me and Gracie; after all, we've got to get all the way to Gorebreath and back. But it's not far from here to Wadingburn; Gubble can meet us there."

"Urk!" There was no doubt that Gubble was sure.

Gracie was still not convinced. "But what about the dogs?"

"Gubble bite. Then dogs do what Gubble says," Gubble informed her, and there was a look in his little piggy eyes that made Gracie decide not to argue anymore.

She turned to Marlon instead. "Is there time for us to go to Gorebreath? Shouldn't we go to Wadingburn Palace straightaway?"

Marlon considered this idea. "The witch won't show her cards till tonight. Get there too early, and you could blow it. Need to play it cool, kiddo."

"OK," Gracie said, but she sounded anxious.

"Don't worry, kid." Marlon winked reassuringly. "I'll see ya there! Oh—almost forgot." He fished under his wing, produced the white peacock feather, and handed it to Marcus. "See you at Wadingburn. *Ciao!*" And he was off and away before the startled prince could offer a word of thanks.

Chapter Twenty-six

Prince Arioso of Gorebreath was striding to and fro in a state of agitation. He had eaten two breakfasts, one as himself, and the other in the role of Marcus, and it had not gone well. He had forgotten that Marcus always talked with his mouth full and slopped his tea, and both King Frank and Queen Mildred had begun by commenting on his much-improved table manners and ended by being suspicious. He had had to upset the teapot in order to escape detection, and he felt cheated. And now the time was passing, and there was still no sign of his brother—and he had no idea what he should do. The royal coach was leaving for Wadingburn in not much more than an hour, and if Marcus wasn't safely inside, Arry was certain his mother would have hysterics and his father would probably call out the army.

He went to look out the window for the fiftieth time — and froze. At the far end of the drive that swept up to the Royal Front Door was . . . Arry screwed up his eyes to see better. "That's Marcus's pony," he thought, "but there's a girl riding it, and she's wearing . . . pajamas! And there's Marcus — whatever is he up to? Oh — he's going to the stables." Arry watched Marcus turn off the driveway and waited anxiously to see what would happen next.

It was a long wait; Arry could not know that Marcus was settling Glee in his stable and arguing with Gracie. "It'll be all right," he assured her. "Really it will. We can go in through the kitchen. I often sneak in that way."

Gracie shook her head. "I'm sorry, but I'm staying here. I can't possibly walk into a palace looking like this."

Alf agreed. "You never get heroines in pajamas in the stories. No way."

Marcus, outvoted, admitted defeat. "I'll get you a dress, then, and bring it here. Mother's got loads — she'll never notice if I take one. I'll be back in two ticks."

Gracie opened her mouth to suggest that it would be really useful to have shoes, and petticoats, and maybe a cloak as well, but Marcus had already vanished. Gracie sighed and sat down on an overturned bucket.

Alf flew up to a beam. "I'll wait here and keep an eye on things, Miss Gracie," he announced as he hung himself upside down.

Marcus arrived in the twins' bedroom panting, having taken the stairs two at a time. "Hi!" he said. "I'm back!"

Arry gave him a reproachful look. "I can see that. Who on earth was that extraordinary girl?"

"Long story, bro." Marcus was hastily flinging off his travel-stained clothes. "Bit of a crisis. Where can I find a dress?"

"What?" Arry stared. "Did you say a dress?"

"Gracie can't go to the ball in pajamas," Marcus explained. "Said I'd find her something to wear. Where does Mother keep her spare stuff?"

"Erm . . ." Arry scratched his head. "I've no idea."

Marcus buttoned up his best velvet coat and headed for the door. "I'll go and have a look. Can you keep an eye out? Keep Mother busy if she comes asking for me. And tell her I'm dressed and ready." The door slammed behind him. A second later it crashed open again, and Marcus reappeared. "Got your peacock feather," he said.

Arry took the feather reverently. "Marcus," he said, "you're amazing. Really amazing."

"I know," his brother said, and was gone.

It was fortunate for Marcus that Queen Mildred liked to take as long as possible getting ready for a party. She was still locked away in her marble bathroom in the midst of warm, scented bubbles, hair curlers, and fluffy powder puffs, having no idea that her son was inspecting the contents of her wardrobe.

"Phew!" he whistled as he looked at the rows and rows and rows of royal dresses. "How on earth do I pick one?" A vague idea crossed his mind that there might be some discrepancy in size between the skinny Gracie and his well-upholstered mother, but he pushed it to one side. "A dress is a dress," he told himself. "Hmm. Blue's nice." And he hauled out an evening gown made of deep blue velvet. As an afterthought he picked up a golden scarf and, pleased with his selection, bundled them into a cloth bag lying at the bottom of the closet.

Hurrying to the stairs, he jumped down and was on his way to the kitchen door when he saw his father coming out of his study. "Oh! Hi, Father! Looking forward to the ball tonight?"

King Frank frowned. "Shouldn't you be getting ready?"

"But I am!" Marcus said indignantly. "Look—best coat, best boots, best everything!"

"You haven't used a hairbrush or washed your face," his father said. "Go back to your room and try again."

Marcus sighed heavily, but knew better than to argue. "If you say so, sir. I'll just run down to the stables and give this to . . . to Ger, and then I'll be straight back."

"You'll go to your room right NOW!" his father thundered. "I'll see you by the front door in twenty minutes, and I'll expect to see you looking like a prince, and not a tramp!"

"Yes, sir." Marcus bowed obediently, but he dashed out the door the second his father was out of sight. Arriving in a rush at the stables, he pushed the bag into Gracie's arms. "Here!" he gasped. "Soon as you're ready, get into the coach. They'll bring it into the yard when they're harnessing the horses. Look out for Ger. Say I said it was OK." And he was gone before Gracie could thank him or ask any questions.

Chapter Twenty-seven

Truda Hangnail had had a good night's sleep and had awoken late. She spent the morning sending the increasingly nervous Mrs. Cringe running to and fro between the hayloft and the small wooden shed where the other witches had been forced to take shelter, the dairy being much in use.

"Someone'll see me for sure," Mrs. Cringe whined, but her grandmother was without pity and sent her away with yet more instructions. It was on her return journey that Mrs. Cringe heard a shriek from the kitchen.

"RATS! I'm sure I saw a rat! Down there by the dresser. Girl—did you see it?"

There was a tiny pause, and then, "Loobly no did see ratty. No ratty be here, missus. . . ."

Mrs. Cringe froze. Loobly. Wasn't that the name of the skinny little runaway orphan? She waited another moment, but hearing nothing other than the clanging of saucepans, she scurried to the hayloft to report to Truda. Malice raised his head at the news, and the old witch's nose sharpened. "Loobly? That's the Trueheart!" Her green tongue flickered as she turned around and around. "There's no taste of Trueheart. Only rat, and they're everywhere. Sure you heard right?"

Mrs. Cringe nodded. Above her head, balanced on a narrow roof beam, Bodalisk kept very still.

Truda snapped her bony fingers. Hundreds of tiny purple wasps zinged around and around the hayloft, and she gave her granddaughter a cold look. "See? See how my spells are working? You must have gotten it wrong. Do the little witchy women know what they have to do?"

"Oh, yes, Grandma. They'll be ready to let in the rats, just as you told them." Mrs. Cringe hesitated. "Are you sure you're not making a mistake? Once they're back to their proper size, won't they turn on you?"

Truda Hangnail smiled nastily. "I'll tell you a secret," she said. "As soon as they've opened the doors and the windows, I'll shrink them again." Her eyes glittered, and she cracked her knuckles in glee. "They'll shrink and shrink until they're no bigger than beetles. And then what'll I do? Step on them, that's what! I'll crush them! Squish them and squash them! Queen Truda of Wadingburn wants no other witches around!"

"Oh!" Mrs. Cringe felt a cold chill spreading through her veins. "Er . . ."

Her grandmother sneered. "Worried, are you? Thinking of yourself? You'll have to wait and see, won't you? Just make sure you do as you're told!"

"Of course, Grandma," Mrs. Cringe whispered, and she huddled in a corner.

Malice licked his lips with pleasure at her discomfiture, then paused. Did he detect a hint of Trueheart? A wasp whined past him, and he snapped at it, missing Truda's ear by a fraction.

"Down," his mistress hissed, tweaking his tail.

Malice glowered and decided to keep his information to himself. The wasp, suddenly aware of danger, flew through a crack in the wooden walls, buzzed across the yard, and whizzed in through the open kitchen window.

"Ooooh! It's a horrid hornet!" The boot boy picked up a dishcloth and began flapping it wildly. "I hates hornets!"

Looby glanced up from polishing teaspoons. "Please not to sting boy," she said quietly, and a blue butterfly swirled away from the dishcloth and drifted across the ceiling.

The boy swiveled around and around. "Oi! Where's that dang hornet gone?"

"Hornet? There's no hornets here." The cook marched toward the door and opened it. "Make yourself useful and help that pretty butterfly out into the sunshine—EEEEEEEEEGH!" Her scream made everyone in the kitchen jump. "A rat! I've seen a rat! Running out of the hayloft, bold as brass . . . Quick, Tommy, quick! Fetch a trap!"

Chapter Twenty-eight

Gracie couldn't decide whether to laugh or cry. The blue velvet dress was at least seven sizes too large, which meant that it successfully covered her bedroom slippers but had a worrying tendency to slide off her shoulders. After some experiments, she twisted the golden scarf into a belt, knotted it tightly, and hoped for the best.

Alf, woken up to see the finished effect, was realistic: "You need to be MUCH fatter, Miss Gracie." And then, worrying that he had been rude, he added, "But it's better than pajamas."

There was a rumbling noise in the stable yard, and he flew out to see what was going on. A golden coach was being rolled out of a large shed and, as Alf watched, six white horses were backed into place and harnessed up. Ger, the stable boy, caught sight of Alf and winked; he was used to seeing bats flitting in and out of the palace. He was far more surprised when a skinny girl draped in yards of blue velvet appeared out of Glee's stable to make her way to the coach.

"Prince Marcus said it was OK if I got a ride with you," the girl said. "Are you Ger? He said to look for you."

Ger, trying not to smile at the sight of bedraggled bedroom slippers under the velvet, bowed and opened the coach door. Gracie climbed in and managed to arrange herself so that most of the surplus velvet was underneath her, and she looked almost passable.

"Very nice, my lady," Ger told her.

Gracie grinned, despite the fact that her stomach felt as if it were tightly packed with blocks of ice. "Thanks."

There was a shout, and Ger vanished. A moment later the coach lurched as the coachman took his place. He shook the reins, and the horses trotted away up the drive toward the palace. As the coach stopped outside the front door, Gracie held her breath.

Marcus bounded up at once. "Here we are, Mother," he said loudly as he swung the door open and peered in to check that Gracie was inside. His eyes widened slightly when he saw her, but he made no comment. "Mother! We're giving Gracie Gillypot a lift; you remember I told you? Queen Bluebell asked her to come—in fact, she wants Gracie to sit next to her."

Queen Mildred, whose wide skirts only just allowed her to enter the coach, was far too preoccupied to say anything except, "Yes, yes! Delighted to meet you, my dear." She sat down with a sigh of relief and was quickly followed by King Frank and Arioso.

"Very pretty dress, Gracie dear," King Frank said gallantly. "Think my wife has one much the same color. Lovely blue, what, what, what?"

"Thank you, Your Majesty." Gracie was aware of Marcus's elbow nudging her in a meaningful way and did her best not to smile.

Queen Mildred, having finally arranged her many skirts to her satisfaction, tapped King Frank on the knee with her fan. "Isn't this *so* exciting?" she said. She turned to Gracie. "We've all been wondering who Queen Bluebell will choose as her successor. Who do you think it will be, my dear?"

Gracie was taken aback by the question. She remembered Edna and Elsie talking about Queen Bluebell but had no clear memory of what they had said. "Erm . . . I don't think I can guess, Your Majesty."

"Of course, I've always hoped her daughter would

miraculously reappear," Queen Mildred said happily. "That would solve the problem nicely. Queen Bluebell the Twenty-ninth she'd be, of course. And then when she had a daughter, that would be Bluebell the Thirtieth. And after that —"

"Mildred! That's QUITE enough!" King Frank tut-tutted and sat back in his seat. "I wouldn't be surprised if Bluebell still hadn't made her mind up. Fine woman — in fact, a very fine woman — but Bluebell's one of a kind. Believes in saying what she thinks and doing what she says. That's why she never got along with her daughter, you know. Both exactly the same; both wanted their own way. Bound to clash."

"Poor dear Bella." His wife fluttered her fan.

King Frank snorted loudly. "Rubbish, Mildred. Nothing poor about Bella. Never wanted to be queen, right from the time she was a baby. Don't you remember? She was always running away from royal parties, always preferred to be in the stables or on the farm. I'd stake my crown she was laughing fit to bust when she left young Vincent on the palace steps, tucked up in a basket with her diamond-buckled shoe. Wish I'd seen Bluebell's face when she found she had a grandson and not a granddaughter. Whoops! Are you all right, Gracie, my dear? You jumped."

"Oh—I'm so sorry," Gracie said. "It was just . . . I just thought of something. It doesn't matter."

"I feel sorry for Vincent." Arioso shook his head. "Poor fellow! Prince of Wadingburn but can't ever be king."

"Hang on a minute! I'm a prince, but I'll never be a king," Marcus interrupted. "But I don't mind. Much rather *not* be king, actually."

"But the new Queen of Wadingburn might be quite delightful, and you could fall in love with her, and the two of you could rule together," his mother suggested.

Marcus made a face. "Not likely. No wonder Queen Bluebell's finding it difficult to choose. There isn't a princess in all the Five Kingdoms that isn't as dull as dishwater."

"Nina-Rose is wonderful," Arry said dreamily.

"Princess Marigold is a sweet little thing," Queen Mildred pointed out, "and so is Princess Evelina . . . or do I mean Charlotte? Or is it Mirabella who has those charming golden curls?" As she began to list the possibilities for future brides, King Frank's eyes closed. Marcus began an argument with Arry over the speed at which they were traveling, and Gracie looked out the window. There was an extremely thoughtful expression on her face.

Chapter Twenty-nine

Brother Bodalisk was not happy. He had risked everything in his dash from the hayloft to the shed, but when he arrived and blurted out the dreadful news Evangeline refused to believe him. "Truda promised she'd let us go," she said. "She absolutely *promised*, just as long as we do exactly what she says. We're to creep into the Royal State Room, where the party's going to begin, and wait until the speeches are over. Then, just as Queen Bluebell is about to declare her successor and everyone's looking at her, we're each to go to a door or a window and—abracadabra! We'll be back to our normal sizes." Evangeline sighed wistfully. "She's even said we won't be whiskery anymore. Won't that be wonderful?"

"Matter of taste," Bodalisk said shortly. "But doll, it's Deep Magic. You can't trust her—"

"But I have to," Evangeline interrupted him. "Don't you see? There's no other way."

"You could stay as you are, babe. The moment I saw you, my heart went pit-a-pat!"

Evangeline shook her head. "I'm sorry, Boddie. Once Queen Bluebell and all her guests see the hundreds and hundreds and *hundreds* of rats, she's sure to make Truda queen — and then Truda'll let us go, and everything will be just fine."

Bodalisk sighed heavily. "Whatever." He took himself off to a corner and slumped against the wooden wall. *Cute babe, Evangeline, but she doesn't care.* A sudden thought popped into his head, and he sat up. *Told that kid in the kitchen I'd let her know what was going on. Might as well do that as hang around here. Kitchen'll be crazy, but do I mind? No. Broken-hearted, that's me.*

And Bodalisk set off down the rat hole that led from the shed to the kitchen.

Marlon was also watching and waiting for an opportunity to speak to Loobly. On arrival at the palace, he had been almost deafened by the noise of the preparations for the party. Servants were running in all directions; one orchestra was tuning up in the grand

ballroom and another on the terrace; and small and flustered pageboys were everywhere, misunderstanding instructions and passing on incorrect messages. Marlon took a deep breath and headed for the kitchen. There he found such chaos that he flew straight out again, followed by loud screams from the cook—but not before he had seen Loobly struggling with a large sack of potatoes.

Flying higher, he investigated other windows. Queen Bluebell the Twenty-eighth was already in the Royal State Room. She was marching up and down, studying a long list of names, looking worried. Prince Vincent was lurking by a side entrance, looking anxious. Various officials, including the Prime Minister, were in their rooms admiring themselves in their mirrors.

Marlon flew higher still. From this height he could see numbers of coaches and carriages all heading toward the palace, although only one or two had gotten as far as the huge stone pillars at the entrance.

"Goin' to be some party," he thought. "That dame may be evil, but she's clever with it. Kings and queens all over the place. If she's declared queen, she'll have Deep Magic in the Five Kingdoms in no time at all." He slipped into a rolling dive and headed back

toward the kitchen. It was still frantically busy, although now the back door was wide open, presumably to cool down the perspiring cook and her assistants.

Marlon grinned and headed for the dairy. With a twist and a spin, he settled himself under the slated roof near a small open window that looked directly onto the kitchen door and prepared to wait.

Chapter Thirty

Gracie was shaken out of her thoughts by the coach going over a series of bumps as they approached Wadingburn. King Frank continued snoring, and Queen Mildred stirred but sank back into a doze. For a moment Gracie wondered why she had a cold, sick feeling at the pit of her stomach—and then she remembered. She was on her way to meet Deep Magic in a dress seven times too large for her, armed with not much more than a wild idea and the crones' belief in the power of Truehearts.

Think positive, Gracie, she thought. *You've got Marcus with you, and Marlon's already at the palace. Oh, and there's Alf as well.* The thought of Alf made her smile, and Marcus winked at her.

"Well done!" he mouthed. "You look . . . OK."

"I can't get out of the coach until your parents have gone," Gracie whispered back. "If I get up, this dress is likely to fall off."

Arioso, ever the Perfect Prince, looked at her in horror, but Marcus leaned forward.

"Listen, bro. There's things going on at the palace, and if you don't want Wadingburn to be overrun with Deep Magic, you'll help us."

"Deep Magic?" Arry paled. "We should tell Father at once——"

"*No!*" Marcus hissed so loudly that King Frank grunted and opened one bleary eye.

Gracie put her finger to her lips, and a moment later the snores continued.

"He'd never believe you," Marcus went on. "You'll just have to trust us. Gracie——Gracie's kind of special. We're on a mission to save the kingdom!"

Arry still looked doubtful.

"It's true, Prince Arioso," Gracie said earnestly. "And . . . and if you could arrange it so your parents get out of the coach before me, I'll . . . I'll be your friend for life."

Arry melted. "I'll do my best," he promised.

"Thank you so much." Gracie smiled her widest smile, and Marcus found himself feeling inexplicably annoyed with his twin. Before he could say anything, however, the coach gave a sudden lurch and stopped.

"The Royal Palace of Wadingburn!" announced the coachman, and King Frank and Queen Mildred awoke with a start.

"Goodness!" Queen Mildred fluttered her fan. "Here we are already! How delightful! Now, children, you get out first. I have to take my time. . . ."

Before Gracie could panic, Arry leaned toward his mother. "Please excuse us," he said, "but Marcus, Gracie, and I have arranged to drive around to the side door to meet Prince Vincent. Would you like me to help you before we go?"

His mother tapped his cheek with her fan. "I'll manage, dear. We'll see you later!" She took King Frank's arm and heaved herself onto the palace steps, where a row of footmen were waiting. "Drive on, coachman!"

Inside the coach, Marcus frowned. "You shouldn't have come with us, Arry," he said as they moved off again. "You'll only get in the way."

"But it's true!" Arry looked affronted. "I arranged to meet Vincent when I saw him yesterday. He's scared his grandmother's going to ask him to make a speech, so he's keeping out of sight, and he wants me to keep him company."

"Oh." Marcus shrugged. "Sorry."

"No offense taken," said his brother grandly, and the coach stopped for the second time.

Before either Arry or Marcus could move, the door was wrenched open, and Prince Vincent was looking in on them. "Arry, is that you?" he asked, and his voice was shaking. "I've just had the most awful shock! I was waiting for you, and I was walking up and down, and I happened to look down through the grating into the cellar, and it's just *swarming* with rats! Millions and millions and *millions* of them! And they weren't just running around—they were in *lines*! And their eyes were all kind of stary and mad—"

"Let me look!" Marcus was already beside Vincent. "Where's this window?"

"Oh . . . it's you, Marcus." Vincent sounded less than enthusiastic. "Erm . . . over there." And he pointed to an iron grating at the bottom of the wall.

"I'm coming too," Gracie said, and with some difficulty she extricated herself from the coach. Vincent's mouth opened wide as she climbed down the steps, and he looked at Arry for an explanation.

"This is Gracie Gillypot, Vincent," Arry explained. "We gave her a lift."

Marcus was bent double trying to see into the cellar,

but before Gracie could join him, he stood up again. "Sorry, Vince," he said. "Must have been a trick of the light or something. There's nothing there—nothing at all."

"What?" Prince Vincent flew to check, then came away shaking his head. "But I *saw* them. I did! I'm sure I did. . . ."

"It's very dark in the cellar," Gracie said kindly. "I often imagine I see things when it's dark."

"I suppose you could be right," Vincent agreed, grateful for the excuse. "Erm . . . forgive me, but isn't that dress just a little too big for you?"

"It's *much* too big," Gracie agreed. "But—but there wasn't much choice." She put her hand on Marcus's arm. "Shouldn't we be going to find the kitchen?"

"The kitchen?" Prince Vincent looked at her in astonishment.

A flash of inspiration hit Marcus, and he nodded. "Don't you remember, Vince? You were telling us all about the amazing cakes for the party. Gracie—Gracie wants to see them!"

"Oh!" Vincent beamed at Gracie. "Of course! There's the most divine sponge with rose-petal cream, and of course the birthday cake is just amazing!" He rubbed his hands together. "And guess what? It's hollow! Can you keep a secret?"

Gracie nodded.

Vincent's smile grew even wider. "I'm going to hide inside, and when Grandmother cuts it open, I'm going to pop up and sing a birthday song!"

"Wow." Gracie could think of nothing else to say. But Arry shook his head. "Won't do, Vincent. Most undignified. Besides, you're the host! Can't leave your guests while you hide in a cake."

Vincent looked sulky. "But I don't want to have to make a speech."

Prince Arioso of Gorebreath drew himself up to his full height and looked disapprovingly at the little prince. "Vincent," he said, "a prince has responsibilities. And a prince has duties. Do you want your grandmother to take you seriously or not?"

Prince Vincent shuffled his feet. "No need to give me a lecture," he said grumpily. "OK. I'll ditch the cake idea. But if we're going to be so responsible and boring and grown-up, then we'd better go straight to the Royal State Room."

"A good decision." Arry took Vincent's arm. "We'll go together. Marcus, Gracie, are you coming?"

Marcus looked at Gracie, and she gave a tiny shake of her head.

"We'll catch up with you later," Marcus said. "You're far more important than we are, Vincent. You go and meet your visitors."

Vincent hesitated. "Are you teasing me?"

"Of course he isn't," Arry said as he marched the little prince away, leaving Gracie and Marcus on their own.

"We'd better look for the kitchen and Loobly," Gracie said. "If we meet her, maybe we could make some kind of plan . . . and she and I should stick together."

Marcus was only half-listening to her. "Gracie," he said, "do you know what? Vincent was right. That cellar was *stuffed* with rats! They were making their way out by the time I saw them, but they were all in rows, just like he said. I didn't tell him, 'cause he'd only have freaked out even more. Where do you think they were going?"

"I don't know." Gracie pulled anxiously at the end of her braid. "I don't like the feel of this place at all. It's giving me the shivers. . . . Let's find Loobly and see what she knows."

Chapter Thirty-one

Truda Hangnail was striding to and fro in the hay-loft, cracking her knuckles and muttering, "Time to get ready. Time to have some fun." She gave Malice's tail a vicious tweak and he snarled, making her cackle with laughter. "The rats will be waiting, and those little witchy women too." She cackled again. "All bright-eyed and thinking I'm going to set them free! Ha!" Her eyes flashed, and Mrs. Cringe, who was cowering by the stairway, shuddered. Truda marched to the window and spread her arms wide. "See that palace? That's all going to belong to me! ME, Truda Hangnail!"

Malice, whose tail was extremely painful, gave a sour chuckle, and the old witch heard him. "What's that? I'll teach you to mock the Queen of Wadingburn!" With a grandiloquent gesture, she flung him away.

"Begone!" she chanted. "Begone!" There was a flurry of purple dust, and Malice sneezed, coughed, choked . . . and disappeared. In his place was a small black beetle, but before Truda could crush him, he scuttled under the hay.

Loobly, sweeping the kitchen floor on the other side of the yard, opened the door to let the dust out. As she did so, she glanced up — and her mouth opened in a silent scream as she saw the witch framed in the hayloft window, wisps of purple smoke surrounding her. Frantically she looked around, her breath catching in her throat and her heart trying to thump its way out of her chest. There was only one place to hide, and she had no time to think what she was doing. When the cook and the other maids came hurrying back from the dining hall, she had vanished.

Truda swung away from the window, unaware that she had been seen. Her eyes were gleaming as she climbed down from the hayloft. At the doorway she stopped, snapped her fingers, and shrank to the size of her quivering granddaughter. "The time has come!" she announced, and after a quick glance left and right, she scurried across the yard and into the shed. Evangeline, Mrs. Prag, Mrs. Vibble, and Ms. Scurrilous were waiting for her, and she greeted them imperiously. "Follow me!" she ordered, and set off down the long, winding tunnel that led to the Royal State Room. The tunnel was curiously empty; not a single rat could be seen.

"They're all in place," Mrs. Cringe promised as they slipped out of the tunnel and under the bookshelves.

"So I should hope." Truda poked Evangeline in the back with a sharp finger. "Get going!"

The Grand High Witch of Wadingburn said nothing as she crept away, followed by Mrs. Prag. Mrs. Vibble and Ms. Scurrilous went in the other direction, and Truda watched until she saw that they were as close to the doors and windows as was possible. Then, and only then, she whisked around and hurried under the shelter of the shelves toward the gilded platform where Queen Bluebell was standing to greet her guests.

Queen Bluebell shivered as she smiled at Queen Mildred and King Frank. "Goose walking over my grave," she said cheerfully, quite unaware that Truda's piercing eyes were fixed on her crown. "What a delight to see you, my dear friends! And are your handsome sons here yet?"

Queen Mildred beamed proudly. "Arioso's over there," she said, "with Prince Vincent."

"Hmph." Queen Bluebell pursed her lips. "Hope

Arioso's talking some sense into him. I love Vince dearly, but he's a silly boy. And where's Marcus?"

King Frank chuckled. "On his way with that little Gillypot girl. She was having a bit of trouble with her dress. Got the wrong size, if you ask me. Not that I know much about these things, of course."

"Excellent!" Bluebell smiled again and turned to her next guests.

Truda cracked her knuckles, and a single purple wasp buzzed around Queen Mildred's head. As the Queen exclaimed and flapped at it with her fan, Truda chuckled darkly.

Gracie was indeed having trouble with her dress. It kept tripping her up and slipping off her shoulders, but she bunched it under one arm and marched gamely on, in what she and Marcus hoped was the direction of the kitchen. Various footmen and upper parlor maids looked at them in surprise and tried to direct them back toward the State Room, but they refused all offers of assistance and kept going.

"It's like a maze," Marcus complained. "Unless we're going around and around in circles. I'm sure that suit of armor's laughing at us."

"Turn left at the next passage, then take the first

right," said a familiar voice, and Gracie clapped her hands.

"Marlon! Oh, where have you been? Where's Loobly? Has the Deep Magic begun?"

"Stay cool, kiddo, and follow me." Marlon fluttered in front of them, and only moments later they were surrounded by steaming pots and pans and facing an agitated red-faced cook.

"'Scuse me, Your Highnesses," she said, "but this isn't the place for you."

Marcus bowed his best bow and switched on his most charming Arioso smile. "I beg your pardon, ma'am," he said. "But might we speak to Loobly? Loobly Higgins?"

"She's gone," the cook said shortly. "Skipped out. Without asking, too. She'll feel my hand when she gets back, I can tell you. And now, if you don't mind . . ." she indicated the kitchen back door and the yard beyond. "You'll find the front entrance just around the corner." Marcus and Gracie found themselves hustled outside, and the door slammed shut behind them.

"Really!" Marcus said indignantly, but Gracie hushed him.

"Loobly is here somewhere," she said. "I know she is. I can't exactly tell you how I know, but I do."

"Trueheart stuff," Marlon said wisely.

Marcus was frowning. "Could she be hiding in the cake? Didn't Vincent say it was hollow?"

Gracie clapped her hands. "Of course!"

"Oi!" The voice was small, and Gracie had to peer into the darkness before she saw the owner. "Oi! What do you want with Loobly?"

"It's a rat!" Marcus stepped backward—but Gracie stayed where she was.

"Hello," she said. "Excuse me, but are you another of Loobly's friends? Like Doily and Sprout?"

"Brother Sprout?" Bodalisk came out into the light. "I know him. One of the brethren. But why're you looking for Loobly? Not another witch, are you?" He studied Gracie carefully. "No. You're like her. You've got that sunshine thing."

Gracie crouched down so that she was nearer Bodalisk's level. "I'm definitely not a witch. I don't like witches. Especially Deep Magic witches."

"So you know what's going on?" Bodalisk came closer still.

"No." Gracie was conscious of a cold feeling in her bones. "Please tell me. I—I might just be able to help."

"That Truda Hangnail. She wants to be queen."

Bodalisk looked at Gracie, and she was reminded of the pleading look in Doily's eyes. "You've got to stop her. You've got to stop her before the Declaration. She's going to blackmail the queen. If you can't stop her, she'll win, and there'll be Deep Magic everywhere, and . . . and then someone I . . . I'm fond of will get squished."

In the distance was the sound of loud clapping, and Marcus froze. "They've started the speeches," he said.

"Quick!" Bodalisk sat up. "HURRY!"

Gracie gulped. "We'd better go."

"But what about Loobly?" Marcus asked urgently. "Didn't the crones say it needed the two of you? We've got to get you together! I'll see if that cook's out of the way." He hurried to the kitchen window. "OH!" he said as he peered inside. "Oh, no . . ."

"What is it?" Gracie asked anxiously.

"They're wheeling the cake out of the kitchen," Marcus said. "She's gone."

Gracie took a deep breath. "We'll have to manage without her." She stooped to scoop up her skirts, and as she did so she heard a tiny squeak.

"Girlie!"

"Doily?" Gracie's eyes opened wide. "Doily? And Sprout as well? What are you doing here?"

"Us is finding our Loobly." Doily's voice was even fainter than usual. "Was longly way with shoe . . ."

"Oh! OH!" Gracie gasped. "Oh, however did you manage?"

Sprout and Brokenbiscuit, covered in dirt and dust and with drooping whiskers, hauled the shoe closer until it rested against Gracie's foot.

"We fetched it for Loobly," Sprout said, and Brother Brokenbiscuit gave a feeble salute.

"You're wonderful," Gracie told them. "This could make all the difference!"

Marcus, who had been anxiously listening to the speeches, swung around. "Gracie," he said, "we really, *really* have to go."

"I'm coming." Gracie picked up the shoe. "Stay close," she told the rats. She took Marcus's hand, and the two of them ran as fast as they could toward the imposing front door of Wadingburn Palace.

Chapter Thirty-two

The Royal State Room was crowded. Truda, who had been amusing herself by sending a couple more tiny wasps whizzing around the room, had already managed to create an atmosphere of some unease. Every so often a king would suddenly duck to avoid being stung, or a queen would stifle a scream as a wasp flew too near. The princes and princesses were finding conversation difficult as first one and then another stopped in mid-sentence to flap a glove or a fan wildly in the air, and tempers were getting ruffled.

As Gracie and Marcus hurried through the door, Queen Bluebell was speaking, her stentorian tones echoing through the room. "It is with much regret that I have to inform you that all efforts to find the natural heir to the throne, namely my daughter, Bluebell, known as Bella, have failed, and I have been forced to accept that she will never take her rightful place as Queen Bluebell the Twenty-ninth. She has been missing now for seventeen years and is, I fear, lost to me forever. Nevertheless, on this, my eightieth birthday, the laws of the kingdom of Wadingburn require a new queen to be named before you all."

Under the platform, Truda took a deep breath of eager anticipation, and the witches of Wadingburn prepared to rush out from their hiding places.

"Dear friends"—Queen Bluebell's voice grew louder—"it is all but time for my Declaration—but first I would like you to celebrate my birthday in the traditional way. Bring in the cake!"

Truda had not expected this, and she began to tap her foot angrily. "Patience, Truda, patience," she told herself. "Let the old bag have a few more minutes."

The double doors behind Queen Bluebell burst open, and an enormous blue-and-white birthday cake was wheeled in, ablaze with candles. There was a burst of enthusiastic applause, and as the orchestra struck up a birthday tune, Queen Bluebell sank into a deep curtsy. The guests sang loudly and enthusiastically until the queen, with one enormous breath, blew out each and every candle, and Prince Vincent shouted, "Three cheers for Grandmother!"

"Thank you, thank you, thank you!" Queen Bluebell boomed, and she picked up a large parchment scroll. "And now—"

"Wait!" screeched a voice. "Wait!"

The guests looked around, startled and alarmed.

"*Aaargh!* It's a RAT!" Princess Marigold pointed with a quivering finger as Truda Hangnail stepped out from under the platform.

"Look again, you little fool," Truda jeered. "Look again!" As she grew taller and taller, the guests shrank back in horrified silence. The witch gave a mocking laugh and strode toward Queen Bluebell, a triumphant smile on her face. "A queen to follow you, that's what you want. And a queen you shall have, for I'm here to take my place. And you'll declare Truda Hangnail queen, or else—"

"Stop!" Gracie came running out of the crowd. "Stop! There is an heir—there is! And I know where!" She rushed to the birthday cake and wrenched away the top layer, revealing the hollow interior.

For a long, long moment, nothing happened, and

then Loobly's pale face emerged. Slowly, as the watching audience held its breath, she stood up and, with Gracie's help, climbed out to stand by Queen Bluebell's throne. When she saw the sea of staring faces, she went pink, and brushed at her grubby apron. "Loobly dirty," she said apologetically.

"No," Gracie said, and she turned to the astonished Queen Bluebell. "Don't you see? Loobly dirty. Seventeen years ago this girl was left on the orphanage steps in a basket with nothing but a shoe — but she'd been taught her name. Loobly Dirty. Bluebell the Thirtieth. Here is the shoe, Your Majesty." Gracie pulled the shoe from her pocket and laid it on the table. "And this is your granddaughter, Bluebell."

"Not so fast, young lady," Truda's lips were drawn back in an ugly snarl. "Not so fast! I've not come this far to be stopped by the likes of you and your fairy stories." She held the bag of bones high above her head and waved it at the doors and windows of the Royal State Room. Purple stars flew in all directions, and Truda chanted, "Open the doors! Open the windows! Let the rats run in! Open the doors!"

The royal visitors, transfixed by fear and incredulity, gasped and whispered and clutched at one another as four more witches rose up, seemingly from nowhere. They moved to the doors, and they moved to the windows, and they opened them wide.

Loobly screamed, "Aunty Levangeline! Aunty Levangeline! Look! My ratty—he no picklified no more. Look!" She brought out a rat from her pocket and held him up . . . and the incoming sea of rats stopped.

They stopped, and they stared, and they shook their heads in disbelief. "Brother Burwash!" they whispered. "Brother Burwash!"

The rat opened his eyes, shook his head, and slipped out of Loobly's arms to the back of the throne. Then he spoke. "Listen here, guys. This won't do. Won't do at all. The young lady's done a lot for me, and I don't want you spoiling her day. Seems as if she's something special, so I'd like you to just run away and—"

"No! No! NO! NO!" Truda raged, and she took her bag of bones and tore it open. Flurries of purple powder swirled into the air, spiraled into eddies, twisted into strange shapes of grinning imps and dancing demons and roaring dragons, while the kings and queens and princes and princesses cowered down, whimpering and moaning . . . and then it was gone.

Nothing was left but a cloud of the palest blue butter-flies, which flittered this way and that before settling on Loobly's arms and shoulders and dress, so that she had every appearance of being dressed in shimmering blue satin. Truda Hangnail, clutching at the throne, gave a feeble moan and began to shrink. Down and down and down she went, smaller and smaller and smaller . . . until she was the size of a rat. Then a mouse. Then a beetle. Then . . . she was gone.

"Wow!" breathed Gracie. "WOW!"

Brother Burwash, his dignity a little impaired by the butterfly sitting on his head, marched briskly toward the goggling rats. "Come along, guys," he said briskly. "Don't want to be intrusive, do we? Think the young lady'll be OK now." He turned and made Loobly a deep bow. "Any time I can be of service, miss, just call me. Brother Burwash, leader of the rats. And I'll make sure you're never bothered by us again, miss. We'll be out of sight. Rat's honor!" And with a cheery whistle, he marched his army away.

There was a long silence, broken at last by Queen Bluebell. "Goodness gracious me." Her voice shook, and she pulled a large handkerchief out of a capacious pocket and wiped her eyes. "Goodness me."

She picked up the shoe and put it down again. "It's the mate to the shoe that Vincent came with. Bella's shoe. Bluebell, my dear, I'm so *very* glad to meet you. Welcome home."

Loobly looked at her grandmother in wonder. "You truly be my grandma?"

"I truly am," Queen Bluebell said, tears running down her cheeks. "I very truly am. Might . . . might you feel able to give your grandma a hug?"

As Loobly was swept into Queen Bluebell's arms, there was a loud and happy sigh from the watching crowd, followed by massive applause.

"It's a real happy-ever-after," said a small voice in Gracie's ear.

"*Alf!*" she said, startled. "Where have you been?"

"Unc says I'm his true successor," the little bat announced proudly. "Look who I've brought here." He waved a small wing. The double doors behind the throne burst open once more, and the dumbfounded guests were treated to the sight of a squat green troll hauling a sullen Buckleup Brandersby behind him.

"Bad man," Gubble announced.

"It's a troll!" Prince Vincent shrieked. "Call the guard!"

"Absolutely not." Marcus stepped forward as Gracie

ran to Gubble's side. "*This* is the man in charge of the orphanage where Loobly was brought up. *This* is the man who kept her in a washhouse. . . ."

There was no need for Marcus to explain any more. As Loobly screamed and hid behind Queen Bluebell, the queen held up her hand. "Take the horrible man away," she ordered. "He will be dealt with later." She sank back onto her throne, holding Loobly tightly as Buckleup Brandersby was pried from Gubble's unwilling grasp. "My poor child. My poor child."

But Loobly was smiling. "Look!" she said. "Look! Is orphans!"

And it was true. Spilling through the doors were the orphans, led by Letty. "Hi, Loo," she said, and grinned. "We came to see you! The troll said there was a party. Said we should come."

Queen Bluebell rose to her feet. "If you are friends of my granddaughter, you are all most welcome," she said. "And you will continue to be welcome. My granddaughter will have a great deal to learn, and it would, I am sure, be a comfort to her to have you here with her."

"'Scuse me," said the smallest orphan, "but does that mean we can eat that cake?"

"The cake and much, much more," Queen Bluebell

told him, and with a loud yelp of joy the smallest orphan hurled himself into the middle of the icing.

Loobly tugged at her grandmother's sleeve. "Is to truly stay here?" she asked.

"Truly is, my dear," Queen Bluebell told her.

Loobly's smile filled the room. "Is *good*," she said happily.

Chapter Thirty-three

Queen Bluebell's guests were mopping their brows and readjusting their crowns as they were marshaled away from the State Room and into the banqueting hall. The orphans were systematically destroying the birthday cake, and it was felt they were best left to get on with it. Plates of healthier and more substantial food were being organized, but for the time being, cake was what they wanted. Gubble was supervising them, aided by Alf and the witches of Wadingburn, with the exception of Mrs. Cringe, who had tiptoed away unseen. Evangeline Droop, who was suffering from a shockingly bad headache, had decided she would leave trying to make sense of all that had happened until another day.

"But perhaps we could assist with the education of these dear children," Ms. Scurrilous suggested.

"Work experience!" Mrs. Prag agreed.

"The preparation of creams and soothing herbs," said Mrs. Vibble. "So very useful."

"We'll think about it," Evangeline said.

The kings and queens were also trying to make sense of what had happened.

"Must have been some kind of play," said one loud voice.

"Of course!" said another, with evident relief. "Of course it was!"

"Splendid stuff, Bluebell old girl!" King Frank marched across and shook the queen's hand. "Never seen anything like it in my life! Good show! Best ever!"

"And *such* a sweet way to introduce your grand-daughter," Queen Mildred said with a sigh. She smiled at Loobly, who was holding Queen Bluebell's hand. "You must come and visit us very soon."

"We'll be delighted," Queen Bluebell told her. "And I'd be most grateful if you could put me in touch with that excellent tutor you had for your boys. Professor Scallio, was it?"

"Of course," Queen Mildred said with a certain doubt in her voice. "Erm . . . you do know his sister is one of the Ancient Crones?"

"And none the worse for that," Queen Bluebell

boomed. "Which reminds me. Where's Gracie Gillypot? Good girl, Gracie. Very good girl. In fact"— she leaned toward Queen Mildred and lowered her voice to a low rumble—"she was the one I'd chosen as my successor. I like her style, and your boy likes her too, doesn't he? Still, things have turned out differently. And she'd probably have hated it. Do help yourself to the chocolate muffins. Delicious, so Vincent tells me."

Gracie Gillypot was not in the banqueting room. Neither was she in the ballroom, where Prince Arioso, an expression of heavenly bliss on his face, was dancing cheek to cheek with Nina-Rose. From time to time the white peacock feather in her hair tickled his nose and made him sneeze, and then Nina-Rose would give him an adoring look and hand him her minute lace handkerchief.

Nor was she in the kitchen, where Prince Vincent was grumpily eating sausage rolls. "A sister," he muttered. "What'll I do with a sister? She looks as if a puff of wind'd blow her away, and I suppose I'll be expected to explain what's what. Teach her how to behave. Show her the ropes and stuff . . . Hmm." He reached for another sausage roll and sat up straighter.

"I suppose I could start with royal etiquette and stuff like that. And it does mean there'll be someone my age around when Grandmother gets in one of her bossy moods. . . . Hmm . . ." He got off the draining board and smoothed his hair. "Maybe it won't be so bad after all. I'll go and see how she's getting on."

As Vincent left the kitchen, there was a rustling from under the dresser. "He's gone," Bodalisk announced. "Coast's clear. Come on, you guys. You deserve a feast." He crept out, followed by Doily, Sprout, and Brother Brokenbiscuit. "Here." He pushed a golden crust of pastry toward Doily, but she shook her head.

"Will us see our Loobly soon?" she asked plaintively.

"Our Loobly's going to be a queen," Sprout said gently. "She won't have time for the likes of us, Doily."

Doily sniffed. "But I do so be missing her."

Bodalisk gave her a sympathetic look. "Know how you feel, doll. Lost my one true love, I have. Gorgeous, with wonderful whiskers—and now she's five foot eleven, and she'll never look at me again. Still . . . life has to go on."

"Shh! There's a Large One coming!" Brokenbiscuit scuttled back under the dresser, but Doily stayed where she was, her whiskers trembling with excitement.

"Is my Loobly!" she whispered, and a moment later Loobly, towing Queen Bluebell behind her like a small skiff towing a battle cruiser, came into the kitchen.

"Here I was working," she explained—and then she saw the rats.

The next few minutes left Queen Bluebell bewildered as Loobly cooed and kissed and hugged and cooed again. At the end of it, the Queen asked, somewhat faintly, "Do you have *many* friends who are rats, my dear?"

"Only mostly," Loobly rocked Doily in her arms. "Ratties are good and kind to Loobly. More kindly than Large Ones. . . . But you be nicely Large One, Grandma."

"Harrumph." The queen shook her head. "Poor child. Poor child. You'd better bring them back with you. Our guests will be wondering where we be. I mean, are. And I still haven't found Gracie Gillypot and that prince of hers. Owe her a lot, from all that I've heard this evening."

But Gracie Gillypot was sitting on the front doorstep of Wadingburn Palace, her blue velvet skirts spread out around her.

"Are you sure you don't want to dance?" Marcus asked. "I really don't mind if you'd like to."

Gracie grinned. "I don't think I'd exactly fit in with all those princesses. They . . . they're . . ."

"Silly." Marcus nodded. "You're absolutely right." He leaned back to look up at the stars, and something in his pocket rustled. "Hey! I'd almost forgotten. I brought my map with me. I was going to ask you. There's a strange little place called Flailing, and it's near where you live. Near the House of the Ancient Crones. Prof. Scallio told me once you can sometimes see dwarfs there, if you're very, very quiet. Would you like to have a look?"

"WOW!" Gracie's eyes shone. "Sounds good to me!"

The prince stood up and stretched. "I'm an idiot. If I'd brought Glee with me, we could have gone now."

Gracie sighed. "Wouldn't it be lovely if we could go now? We could go home, have a cup of tea, and tell the crones what's happened. They must be worrying. And then tomorrow maybe we could look for the dwarves."

"You can go right away, kiddo." Marlon swooped over their heads, followed by Alf. "Nothing to stop you."

"What? How?" Gracie and Marcus stared at him.

Marlon pointed. "The path . . . see? You did good, see? House of the Ancient Crones—it's a Trueheart House. Like the path."

And as Marcus and Gracie watched, their eyes growing rounder and rounder, the path came rippling up to tickle their toes.

"Happly after," said a familiar voice, and Gubble came stumping around the corner. With a grunt he climbed on board and patted the path invitingly. "You too. Happly after."

In the House of the Ancient Crones, the Ancient One watched the faint remains of the stain on the web fade into nothingness. "It's gone," she said.

"Well done, Gracie Gillypot." Elsie yawned. "Shall I make some tea?"

"That's an excellent idea," said the wisest of the Ancient Crones. "I've a feeling in my bones that we're about to have company. Is there any cake?"